THE
TOWN TAMER

Center Point
Large Print

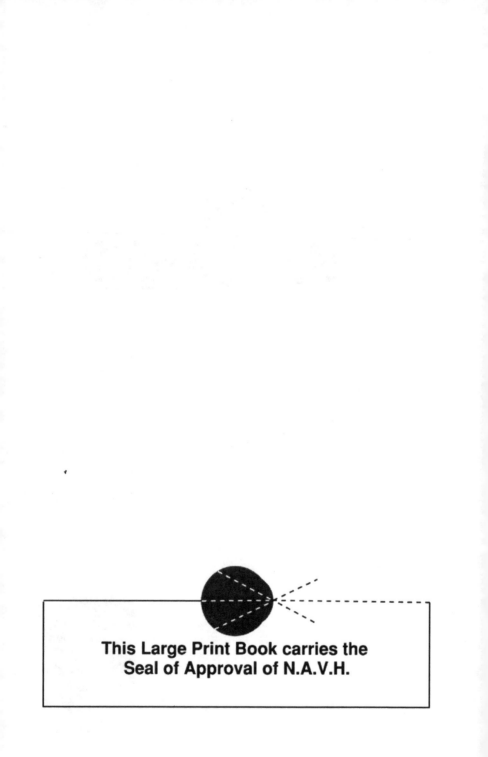

**This Large Print Book carries the
Seal of Approval of N.A.V.H.**

THE
TOWN TAMER

PARKER BONNER

CENTER POINT LARGE PRINT
THORNDIKE, MAINE

Library of Congress Cataloging-in-Publication Data

Bonner, Parker, 1903–1980.
The town tamer / Parker Bonner. — Center Point Large Print edition.
pages cm
ISBN 978-1-62899-737-8 (hardcover : alk. paper)
ISBN 978-1-62899-742-2 (pbk. : alk. paper)
1. Large type books. I. Title.
PS3503.A5575T69 2015
813′.54—dc23
                                        2015028542

THE
TOWN TAMER

CHAPTER ONE

It was raining: a hard, high mountain storm that blinded the two riders and their horses. These summer deluges broke quickly and quit abruptly, but while they lasted no man in his right mind stayed in the saddle if there was the least shelter to be had.

The community of Smith's Crossing was deserted, the old buildings abandoned to whatever animals might choose to use them. Doors sagged half open on rusting hinges. Windows with no panes showed briefly as black, hollow eyes in the swift, jagged flashes of lightning.

Bart Layton, bent forward, his head down against the driving wet, led the race toward the dark hulks. He splashed through the mud of the old inn yard with Dugan cursing at his heels.

The runway of the wrecked stable was dry. They rubbed the animals down, shoved them into the bare box stalls, then made a run for the main building, rain sluicing off the tails of their ponchos.

Inside the echoing cavern that had been the barroom Layton dug through his pockets for a match still dry enough to strike, and with the little flame held over his head made a quick survey. The bar mirror was cracked, the floor strewn with broken bottles, glasses, refuse dragged in by industrious pack rats.

One of the wall lamps, dust covered, still sat in its metal bracket, its chimney miraculously intact, its glass bowl half full of yellowing kerosene. He turned up the wick, lifted the chimney, rubbed the old char with his match. He watched it catch, the light begin to swell, dropped the match as his wet fingers scorched. He scrubbed some of the dust from the chimney onto his soaked pants, then replaced it. As the yellow glow probed into the remote corners he pivoted slowly, looking around the old room. He was smiling to himself, humming, a lean, blue-eyed blond with a rakish poise that suggested wind around him.

His tune was drowned under Dugan's rhythmic, monotonous blasphemy. Dugan, stopping just inside the door to sweep off his hat, fling the water from it, was blocky, only five feet ten, with wide shoulders and a bull neck running up into his round bullet head. The mark of the service was on him—in the way he stood, spine straight, shoulders back; in the way he walked, the stiff gait of a man more used to riding.

"Christ, what a dump." He took in the litter, the broken tables, the overturned chairs. "Must have been one hell of a fight here a long time ago."

Layton's smile spread, wide and quick. "A lot of fights, Sarge, a whole lot. When I was a kid we rode down here to raise hell every Saturday night regular."

"We're finally that close to Montrose, Captain?"

"Only three, four more miles. We'll ride on in as soon as this shower's over." He shivered as a gust of wind blasted through the door. "Chilly, this high up. I could use a drink. Shame they didn't leave just one bottle whole."

Mike Dugan grinned, a wide twisting of his thin lips. His weathered face was craggy, his nose canted to the right in commemoration of some old fight of his own. Grinning, he had a glow like a bare mountain catching full sunlight. He wrestled a flat bottle from under his poncho, held it forward. It was half full.

"Guess we don't need to keep this any more for snake bite."

Layton came forward, a long, lean brown hand reaching. The raw whiskey burned down to his flat stomach. He checked the level left in the bottle. It was still above his thumb. He drank again, passed the bottle back to Dugan. Dugan emptied it and tossed it at another bottle on the floor. Both of them shattered with an almost musical spray of sound. He wiped his mouth with the back of his hand.

"Feels kind of empty to know I don't have to stand guard tonight."

"It was your choice."

"Sure it was. Sure. What I mean is, the army's

like a woman. You give it twenty years of your life and all you got left is memories." He spat thoughtfully, solemnly on the floor. "Damn Custer anyhow for a glory hunter. Little tin soldier playing God. He'll get a lot of good men killed before he's through. But you didn't have to hit him, Captain. You didn't have to hit him."

Layton's mouth turned down, but in spite of himself the memory forced it up again.

"It was worth it, Mike. He rode me from the time he joined the regiment. I was just lucky nobody else was around, Georgie couldn't have stood it if his newspaper friends had found out. He still thinks he's a general. He was damned glad to have me resign. A court-martial might have brought up a lot he wouldn't want to see in print. But you didn't need to buy out."

"It wouldn't have been the same." Mike Dugan's head shake was morose. "Besides which, how was you going to make out with me not around to take care of you?"

"I told you, I'll be all right. I was raised in Montrose. My grandfather owns the mine up there."

Mike Dugan's eyes widened. "You never said that. If your family's so all-fired rich, what were you doing hiding in the army?"

Layton shrugged impatiently. "We didn't get along. In his own way the old man's a bastard. Whatever he gave you, you had to beg for, and I wasn't any good at that. I left the begging to my cousins. When I was seventeen he tried to use a whip on me. I took it away from him and gave him a couple of licks, just so's he'd know how it felt. Then I cleared out."

"Captain, you are the damnedest for sure. First you whip your grandpappy and then you go and swing on Custer. Didn't anybody ever tell you there are some people in this world you just don't hit?"

"Like sergeants, maybe? How about that sergeant from K that got his arm broke?"

Dugan backed water virtuously. "Well now, about that . . . he called me an Orangeman. He had to be showed his place."

"So my grandfather called me a snot-nosed brat and Georgie told me I was a first-class S.O.B. Who else shouldn't we hit?"

Dugan lifted and dropped his shoulders. "You had to get out of the army when you didn't want to, and you had to leave your rich grandpappy. What's he going to say when you ride back in— *welcome home, prodigal, all is forgiven?*"

"It will be interesting to see. He just might set the mine police on me. He's been boss of the Gabriel Mine for so long he thinks he's God. Just like Custer."

Dugan had been kicking through the litter, scowling at the broken window through which the storm still raged. He turned like a panther, surprisingly quick for one of his build.

"The Gabriel Mine?"

"Yeah. When he first found the ledge he tried to sell an interest to some money men in Denver. Talking it up, he bragged that the property was so rich it would still be bearing when Gabriel blew his horn. He didn't sell the interest, but stubborn as he was he hung the name on the find."

"The Gabriel. I'll be damned." Dugan sounded bemused.

"What's that supposed to mean? What do you know about the Gabriel?"

Mike Dugan's eyes looked at Layton and through him. He filled his big chest with air and let it out in a soundless whistle.

"You remember, last year when Yantee's patrol got cut off by the Sioux? They killed everyone but Yantee?"

"I was at Schofield picking up replacements."

"So you were. Well, the Indians thought Yantee was dead. They scalped him and left him. Some trappers found him alive and brought him in, but his mind was gone. Tom Custer sent me with a detail to take him to the asylum at Bedford. Yantee's still there, I guess. . . ."

Layton waited. The sergeant was leading up to something relevant, but Layton had learned not to push him.

"Anyhow, I laid over the night before heading back for Lincoln. . . . You ever been in a nutty house, Captain?"

Layton shook his head without speaking.

"It's something, believe me." Dugan shuddered and crossed himself. "Them poor guys. I'd rather have my brains cut out than be the way some of them are."

"All right, all right, get to the point. You're so full of wind."

The way the sergeant looked at him he thought his impatience had scattered the rest of the story, that he'd never hear it. Then Dugan was talking again, lower, portentous.

"That's right, Captain, that's right. But you just listen. There was an old fellow there in a wheelchair, pretty much crippled up. A guard pointed him out to me, said he'd been in a mine accident, that he'd rescued a dozen miners and that a timber fell on him. The guard used him like a showpiece, saying he'd been the richest man in the territory, that he'd owned the Gabriel Mine."

The blond captain stared. "Are you telling me Ryan Layton is in an insane asylum? Why didn't you say so before?"

Mike Dugan spread his thick-palmed hands. "What was to say? I didn't know his name, just that it seemed a hell of a thing for somebody like him to be strapped to the arms of a wheelchair. You never mentioned any Gabriel Mine before. . . . It's kind of strange that nobody wrote and told you."

Bart Layton's voice was rasping, dry. "Not so strange. No one in Montrose knew where I was."

CHAPTER TWO

The mining town sprawled over the flat floor of a wide canyon. Along the base of the steep north wall ran Montrose Creek, flooding now from the recent storm. The roar of its galloping waters joined with the pound and whine of the hoisting engines at the mine perched high above.

A single street bisected the bending canyon, a five-block cluster of business buildings strung on it like beads, single-story, false-front structures facing each other across the churned dirt road. Behind them houses sat at independent angles as if each builder had deliberately refused to conform to his neighbor's ideas. There were no side streets or back streets, only twisting paths winding uncertain ways, connecting the houses by their web.

The main road caught and held the runoff water of the valley. It was a yellow soup now and the horses slopped through it knee deep, not liking it.

Most of the town was dark, but a lamp burned in the livery office and Layton turned up into the wide runway, bringing mud onto the packed earth floor and the litter of loose hay.

As he stepped down a man came from the office, an old man, rubbing sleep from red rimmed eyes with dirty knuckles, his body bent as if he wore a pack on his back. He met his customers without pleasure.

"Turn them into the corral out back."

The voice was reedy with the quaver of age, and the man made no gesture to help. They pulled off the wet saddles, the sodden blankets, led the animals on through to the mud again, shoved them within the stout fence. The hostler had retreated again to the office by the time they returned. He was settled in the broken rocker where he slept out most of his night shift. He did not look up as Layton stopped in the doorway.

"Staying long?"

"Don't know, Andy."

The old eyes opened in a squint, taking in the broad shoulders under the poncho, the thin face and beak nose that made Layton look like a hungry eagle, the soggy campaign hat.

"Say . . . I know you. . . ."

"You ought to, Andy. You taught me how to shoot."

"Bart Layton? Where the hell did you drop from?" His eyes had settled on the hat. "Heard once that you was in the army. Old Ryan heard it too, like to had a fit, he did, him being from Carolina."

"I'm out now." Layton took off the hat. "That's all I got left, Andy. Couldn't find a hat at the sutler's to go with my new clothes."

"Well now. Well." The old man was fitting

15

himself to his surprise. "Things do change. Reckon you heard about your grandpaw?"

Layton glanced at Dugan, watching silently. "What about him?"

The barn man spat philosophically. "Funny how things work out. The old bastard did one decent thing in his miserable life. There was an explosion at the mine two years back . . . seven men got trapped and nobody wanted to go in after them. So whatd'ya know, Ryan Layton went into that tunnel alone. He got them out too, all but one. He was dragging that one when a beam fell across his back. That shamed the crowd into helping then, and they got Ryan loose, but his back was twisted like a pretzel. It healed, but he was in a wheel chair from then on."

"Where is he now?"

The old man scratched his hand through his thin hair. "In the nut house over at Bedford."

"Why?"

"Well, there's all kinds of stories, you know how these mountain towns talk. . . . You remember Mary Dorne? School teacher?"

Layton shook his head and Andy spat again. "No, I guess you'd hightailed before she come out from the east. Well, she quit her job and moved into your grandpaw's place to take care of him. Seemed to work fine for awhile. He appeared to be all right, cranky as hell, but then he always was mean as a badger. Then one day he tried to kill her."

"Kill her?"

"Yes sir. She was bending over his chair getting ready to help him to bed. He grabbed her hair with one hand. He had a knife, guess he got it from the kitchen, and he was going to cut her throat. She fought free, left a lot of hair in his fingers. Sheriff found it still there when the neighbors heard her yells and called him."

Bart Layton's eyes were narrowed, skeptical. "Sounds hard to believe, Andy. You and I know he could be mean in a business deal and to me and my cousins, but I never heard him raise his voice to a woman."

"Yep. Folks figured he got hit on the head when that beam came down. Doctor said he talked a lot of foolishness when they carted him down to the courthouse jail. Judge finally committed him. Wasn't much else he could do."

"Who's running the mine?"

Andy scratched his head again. "That's a nice question. The judge appointed your cousins as trustees. Them and Caleb Hewmark have been running things. Remember him?"

"Denver."

"That's right. Seems he loaned your grandpaw a quarter of a million to keep the mine going. The mill returns haven't been so good the last few years. He took a quarter interest for his loan. Tell you what, the way I see it the Gabriel is about worked out. Town's slipping. Lot of people moved

17

out last year. Mine's only working one shift now and there's talk it might close."

Layton thought of the bright picture ore that had been taken from the Gabriel during his childhood. "That's hard to believe."

"Way mines go. More money's been poured into the ground than ever was took out. Sorry I'm the one to give you the bad news, boy."

"I'm glad you did, Andy." Layton sounded troubled. "It's always better if a man knows what he's up against." He glanced at Dugan. "Let's go get a room and then a drink. I feel like I could use one now."

He nodded to the barn man and went out to the wooden sidewalk that ran barely above the muddy street. Dugan, beside him, gave an embarrassed laugh.

"Quite a windjammer."

Layton's voice told that his mind was not on his words. "Quite a guy when he was younger. He used to be head of the mine police, then he had a run-in with the old man. He's broken a lot since I saw him last."

The boards were slippery with mud splashed up on them and they picked their way carefully, the thump of their boot heels echoing across the empty block.

They turned in at the lobby of the two-story hotel, found it lighted by a single lamp, turned low, above the high desk. A wall clock beside the key board read twelve-thirty. The clerk slept in a cane chair behind the desk, a sallow man with no chin, his lips bubbling out low snores.

He came awake with a mew of protest, scrubbed sleep from watery eyes with one hand while he turned the ledger. He watched Layton scribble their names, slid a key across the counter and waved a claw toward the stairs. Then he yawned and settled back to sleep.

They climbed the stairs in silence, found the room down a hall filled with heat and dust smells trapped there by the moisture in the outside air. There were two beds, the mattresses thin and lumpy, the springs sagging. Layton tossed his saddle bags on one, Dugan dropped his on the other.

"Let's go get that drink."

Bart Layton stood leaning a little forward, poised on the balls of his feet as if he balanced on a coiled spring. His hands hung at his sides, the fingers idly massaging the heels of his thumbs. His face, empty, still held a shadow of truculence, the eyes wandered over Dugan without seeing him. Dugan understood. The captain might cuss his grandpappy from here to yonder, but nobody likes to think of any of his kin in a crazy house. He thought a fight might develop before the end of the evening, with Layton letting off some steam, and smiled to himself. It might be good for both of them. Then Layton filled his chest and cheeks with air and let it out slowly between barely closed lips.

"Yeah. A drink."

The Palace Saloon abutted against the hotel wall, a big, bright room with swinging crystal lamps reflected in a gleaming backbar.

As a youngster Layton had believed it was the fanciest barroom in the world. He did not see it that way now. It looked smaller. It was certainly meaner. There were gaps in the fringe of hanging prisms, some of which were broken. The floor under the thin spread of sawdust was splintered by spur rowels, embedded with grit from miners' boots. Only half a dozen men were scattered along the dark rolled edge of the bar. Only two poker tables at the rear were occupied.

The bartender was the same, another big Irishman with a face as craggy as Dugan's but red, whiskey burned. He came forward impassive, ready to be friendly or not, a spotted cloth in his hand unnecessarily wiping at the mahogany counter where they stopped.

"Your pleasure?"

Mike Dugan did not see the room through memory. By way of commenting on its low estate he said, "Whiskey. Irish, if you'd have it."

The bartender had sized up the sergeant, recognized him as one of the chosen. He recognized the slur and gave it back in his flat inflection. "We do that."

Dugan's unhidden surprise and pleasure satisfied him.

"Clare."

"Cork."

"It's a good place," said the bartender, "but not so good as Clare." He set three glasses on the bar, searched beneath it, brought up a bottle and poured. "This I keep for my own use. And it's not everyone I'd be drinking with." The glass he lifted half vanished into the heavy walrus mustache, then he squinted at the captain, ignored at Dugan's side. "I've seen you somewhere, lad."

"You have, Terry, a time or two."

"Bart Layton?"

The captain nodded. There was a change in the bartender's eyes.

"I heard you were soldiering."

"I gave it up."

Terry refilled the glasses by feel, his eyes on Layton. "And now you've come home. It's about time. The town ain't what she used to be, lad. She's run way down hill. Way down."

Layton wanted to ask questions, a lot of questions, but a bar was not the place. He limited himself to one. "My cousin Clint still live at the hotel?"

"Aye."

Layton bought another drink, looked to Dugan. "You had enough?"

The sergeant's face widened in astonishment. "With whiskey left in that bottle? That's the first Irish I've tasted in ten years."

Layton's smile was wry. He winked at Terry. "When he gets to where he can't walk throw him in the back room. He's peaceful enough unless you start singing God Save the Queen."

The bartender's mustache spread with his grin. "Anyone sings that in here will have the two of us to fight. Watch yourself, lad." The grin was gone.

On the street the words came back to Layton. *Watch yourself.* Was it a warning or a casual parting. He could think of no one who should worry him in Montrose. As far as he knew he had no real enemies on the mountain.

A heavy odor of stale whiskey hung in the cheerless room around Clint Layton. He had been asleep. He stood holding the door open, blocking it, his paunchy stomach covered with long underwear. He blinked into the light of the hotel hallway.

"What's the matter? What do you want?"

"It's Bart."

His cousin blinked harder. "Bart who?"

"Layton, you damn fool. Let me in."

Clint waddled back a step, watched Bart walk past him, then turned, fumbled for the lamp on the table beside the bed and lit it. In the rising glow his puffed eyes were bloodshot. There was a half bottle of liquor on the scarred dresser, a glass beside it. He poured into the glass, concentrating, drained it at a gulp. His big body quivered as the liquor hit the swollen stomach.

"What are you doing here?"

"I'm out of the army. I've come home."

Clint's laugh was a hollow bellow. "Home. To what?"

Layton kept disgust out of his face. He had not seen this cousin for ten years, and there had been no love between them from the beginning. Clint Layton had been fat when Bart went away. He was gross now. The wattles of his cheeks sagged and his chin hung down into the bulging neck with no clear break along the jaw line. Bart schooled his voice.

"What's this I hear about grandpaw?"

"I don't know what you heard." Clint was pouring himself another drink.

Bart Layton took two quick steps, took the bottle in one hand, the slopping glass in the other and wrenched them free.

"Lay off that until you answer me."

Clint's gray eyes smoldered and color touched the gray tan of his loose cheeks, but no hint of anger came through the thickened voice.

"What do you want to know?"

"I heard Ryan is in an asylum."

"That's right. He tried to cut a woman's throat."

"Ryan Layton?"

Clint sunk down on the edge of the bed, bending it. The fat of his body ran down even to his bare feet.

"You didn't see him after the mine accident. He was goofy as a bedbug. He kept harping that somebody was stealing high-grade ore from the mine."

"Was someone?"

"How the hell could they? The stuff was loaded at the shaft mouth and hauled down to the mill in our own ore carts. Just to quiet him I followed half a dozen of those carts. They none of them made a single stop."

"Did he think he had a reason for attacking the school teacher?"

"School teacher . . . so you've already heard it someplace else?"

Layton nodded. "What about it?"

His cousin threw up his fat hands. "Who tries to explain what a crazy man will do? The doctor examined him, the judge put him away. The people at the asylum have nothing but trouble with him."

"What does he say?"

"I haven't seen him. They won't let us, say it excites him, makes him worse, say he's hard enough to handle without somebody from the outside getting him wrought up. Dick hasn't seen him either."

"Where is Dick?"

"He should be on his way back from Denver by now. Now go on, let me get some sleep."

Layton saw that he would get little more information here. He turned and left the room.

Behind him the fat man stared at the closed door. He rubbed the side of his fleshy nose thoughtfully, then he sighed, rose and began to dress.

CHAPTER THREE

Mike Dugan had found a brother, a man of his own kind. He and Terry Roark leaned across opposite sides of the bar happily trading insults. The bottle of Irish long since empty, they had switched to bourbon, but neither showed any visible effect of their intake.

One poker game broke up, then the second. The night was now clear and the customers drifted out into it. The two Irishmen found they had the place to themselves. They finished the bourbon, put out the lamps. Roark locked the door behind them, locked arms with Dugan and together they rambled down the street, singing. They reached a cross trail and Roark swung into it, his feet automatically taking him toward the three-roomed cabin and his wife.

Dugan hauled up, looked solemnly around,

reconnoitering his position, pounded Roark's shoulder in a fond goodnight and made his way back to the hotel.

He climbed the stairs, humming under his breath, his tread so light that the desk clerk did not stir. His head rose above the floor level of the upper hall just in time to show him a man climbing through the window at the far end.

Dugan stopped. The stairs were in deep shadow. He watched, amused as a second man followed the first. A pair low on funds who wanted to sleep in a bed free. They stood together whispering for a moment, then moved on silent feet and stopped before a closed door. The first man lifted a gun from his holster, put his hand on the knob and softly opened the door.

It came through Dugan's whiskey, stabbing at his mind sharply, that this was his and Layton's door. This was no innocent beating the clerk out of a couple of dollars. The men were gunning for the captain.

All of Mike Dugan's life had been lived in violence. His move now was pure reflex. He took the rest of the steps in a rush, his indignant bellow blasting ahead of him, his feet pounding down the uncarpeted hall.

The first man had already disappeared into the room. The second swung, crouching, his hand clawing at his gun. He did not get it clear of the holster. Dugan's shoulder caught him in the chest, knocked him back against the flimsy wall with a force that shook the frame building.

It did not occur to Mike Dugan to pull his own weapon. He was a rough-and-tumble fighter for the sheer physical joy of fighting. He and Terry Roark had just been reminiscing some of the better of those fights. He slammed his fist into the man's stomach, felt the rush of hot air driven from the other's open mouth. He chopped to the neck, brought up his knee, drove it hard into the man's groin. The man fell down Dugan's trunk and lay writhing on the bare boards.

Dugan spun toward the open door. There was no light inside. He heard Bart Layton's startled voice and the creak of bedsprings. Then the first man's shadow was in the doorway, the gun in his hand reflecting a wink from the hall lamp. The gun exploded inches from Dugan's face. The heavy slug hit the bridge of his canted nose. He was hurled back with a sledgehammer blow.

Dugan was dead before he bounced on the floor.

The gunman pivoted and drove two shots back into the dark room in the direction of the bed. Bart Layton had rolled out, dropped flat at the sound of the first shot. He fumbled under the bed where he had stowed his gunbelt, and both blind bullets went over his head.

He found his gun, dragged it free, fired at the silhouette in the doorway as it jerked away out of sight.

Noise in the rest of the building, curses, shouts, swelled as other tenants waked and tumbled off their beds. The gunman in the hall stooped, yanked his companion to his feet and rushed him toward the open window.

Bart Layton had crawled forward cautiously. He reached the door and peered around the jamb in time to see one figure straddling the sill. His bullet caught the man's side, boosted him outward. Layton heard him hit the slanting shed roof below the window, roll across it, heard the body thud on the ground. He ran, thrusting half through the opening. There was no moon, but enough star glow to show him the sprawled figure. It did not move.

Turning back, he found the hall filling as people spilled out of rooms. Few minutes had elapsed since Dugan's bellow and something crashing against the hall wall had jerked him from sleep. The gun dangling from his hand, he walked slowly back. He saw the room clerk's scared face rise in the stairwell, saw the growing knot of men. Some of them were armed. He had no place to put his gun. He was in his underclothes. But no one challenged him.

He knelt beside Dugan, looking into the ruined face, looking at the mess where the heavy slug had torn away a part of the skull.

Rage, consuming, stifling, burned through him. His had always been a dangerous temper and it threatened now. He fought it, trying to think. Had robbery been intended? He rejected that. Robbery would not explain why the gunman had taken time to fire at a bed he could not see after Dugan's warning roar. Nor was the attack aimed at Dugan, a reprisal for something that might have happened in the bar, for Dugan was in the hall.

He remembered Terry Roark's parting *Watch it,* and the hint in the tone that had made him wonder. It was he they had wanted. He did not know why, but there could be no other answer.

The hubbub was growing. The clerk had come up, nervous, chattering questions. He put a hand lightly on Dugan's still chest, then rose slowly. His rage was not diminished. It was growing, but settling as a white hot ball within him.

Dugan had been more than a friend. The sergeant had taken him under his wing at the time he joined the regiment. He had eased the mistakes that all new officers make, he had saved Layton's life three times. He had fussed with the protective energy of a mother hen.

And Dugan, who had loved the service as another would love a woman, had left the army rather than stay after Layton had resigned.

Bart Layton had seldom cried even as a child. He did not now. But unseen tears stung the backs of his eyes and his throat.

"What happened? What happened?" The clerk's parrot phrase, its monotony, drilled through to

Layton's consciousness. He looked across the crowd, looked at each face individually. There was not one he remembered.

"Someone broke into my room. To kill me."

The eyes stared back, blank, unreadable. He indicated Dugan's body.

"My partner happened along at the time."

He turned back into the room. By the time he had kicked into his damp clothes the sheriff had arrived.

The sheriff was Layton's age. They had grown up together, chased the same girls. Foster was a small man with sandy hair, a pointed nose and blue-green, squinting eyes. He stood beside Layton, over the man who had fallen from the shed roof. There was a streak of light in the eastern sky.

"Know him?"

Foster held a lighted match near the dead man's face. "Name's Hauser. A mucker in the mine."

"Been in trouble?"

The sheriff shrugged. His father had been a shift foreman before he was killed under a cave-in. "Nothing to speak of. Got in a knife fight last year." He pointed to a puckered scar across the left cheek.

"Who'd he fight?"

"Some high-binder that rode in. He got away. We never did find him."

Layton had no memory of either the face or the

name of the mucker. Foster straightened, looking up with open curiosity.

"Who knew you were in town, Bart?"

Layton filled his lungs, emptied them. "Andy over at the livery. The hotel clerk. Terry Roark. Dozen or so men were in the saloon, I didn't pay much attention. Oh, and my cousin Clint."

"Oh?"

Something in Foster's tone drew a quick glance from Layton.

"What's that mean, Fred?"

The sheriff lifted his shoulders. "Nothing. I kind of remembered you and Clint didn't hit it off so well in the old days."

"He was a slob. I never had any real trouble with either him or Dick. It was just that they always sucked around the old man too much for my taste." He thought of something. "That's funny."

"What is?"

"Practically everybody turned out of their rooms when the shooting started, but I didn't see Clint. He couldn't have slept through all that racket."

"Let's go ask him."

They went back into the hotel through the big kitchen. But they did not talk to Clint Layton. He was not in his room. No one remembered seeing him that night.

CHAPTER FOUR

Terry Roark was the only mourner other than Bart Layton at Dugan's burying. The big bartender stood beside the open grave as the undertaker's two men lowered the rough wooden box into the fresh hole. His bowed head was uncovered to the sun as the priest finished speaking, stooped and tossed the handful of dirt on the box top. Then he turned away and walked heavily at Layton's side, away from the grave on the barren, windswept hillside.

"I could have been his friend." He said it to himself, under his breath, the rumbling voice no more than an echo. "It's funny how boys like that have few friends. We're a stupid race, lad. We treat our enemies better than we do our own."

Layton made no answer. He was thinking that Roark's words applied as well to him. This was his town. His father had been killed in a stage-coach accident. He had been born here because of that accident. His mother had died in the birthing. He had been raised with his two cousins by his uncle's wife. Both cousins had been older; they had bullied him until he grew heavy enough to lick them. And he had chosen his friends from the rougher element of the town, miners' sons, boys in trouble, boys who had been rejected as he felt rejected.

As a result, he had been in constant trouble, at odds with his family, resenting his grandfather's domination. Twice he had been arrested for petty theft, once for stealing a suit of clothes when Ryan Layton had refused him money to dress for a dance, once for helping four others roll a keg of beer out of a local saloon.

On this second offense he had been turned over to his grandfather, who had taken a whip to him. He had wrestled the whip from Ryan Layton's hand, used the lash on the mine baron and fled town on a borrowed horse.

Chance could have turned him into the outlaw trail. Instead he had ridden into a stage holdup and by accident had rescued the territorial governor. His reward had been an appointment to the Point. From there he graduated, a second lieutenant, into an army topheavy with officers who had served through the war. Some of them had been in grade for years. Layton could well have waited twenty years without promotion. But fortune had sent him to Fort Grant in time to take part in the early Apache campaigns. He had seen five officers who ranked him killed in as many months and had been promoted by brevet, first to lieutenant, then to captain in only three years.

Had he stayed in Arizona with the company which had been detached from the Seventh ever since the war, he would still be in the army. But Company B had been ordered to Lincoln to rejoin the old regiment. And here he had run afoul of Custer.

He put the thought behind him. Being who he was, what he was, there could have been no other result. In Arizona he had been as near a free agent as ever a junior officer could be. On the southern frontier the commanders were far more interested in a man's knowledge of Indians than they were in the regulations of discipline. The trouble with Custer had come because the former boy general was too certain of his own charisma, unwilling to acknowledge that the Indians he fought were among the greatest strategists of history.

Montrose drowsed in the summer sun. Heat waved up from the dust of the main street, the porous earth already drained of yesterday's soaking.

Before the Palace Saloon Terry Roark stopped and turned to Bart Layton with somber eyes.

Layton said, "Last night I thought you gave me a warning. Do you want to add to it now?"

Roark hesitated. Thirty years behind a bar had taught him caution. A bartender heard much, saw much. A wise one kept his own council. If he stayed in business he took no sides.

"You're a grown man," he said reluctantly. "When you took out of here you were a brash kid. I thought you'd be dead before you turned twenty.

From what Dugan said about you I'm frankly glad you're back. If this town is to come alive again someone will have to do something about the mine. Maybe you're the one. I don't know." His eyes left Layton; he turned and disappeared, the saloon doors flapping behind him as if to cut off all communication.

The street was not as busy as Bart remembered it. Still, it was crowded with ore carts dragging down from the mine, hauling the heavy rock to the noisy mill at the lower edge of town. There were occasional freight wagons bringing in supplies from the railroad, fifty miles away. A stage thundered in, pulled up with a rattle of harness chains and a swirl of dust at the office beyond the hotel.

Layton knew that his passage along the sidewalk was attracting attention. The story of the shooting in the hotel was all over town. Half a dozen men spoke to him. Some he knew vaguely, others did not touch his memory. People changed in ten years.

The bank was a long, low, one-story brick structure, a solid, unlovely box. In other times Ryan Layton had sat at the rolltop desk in the far corner and from its creaking chair directed not only the operation of the mine but half the businesses of the town. Now Blakestone Heath occupied the big chair but did not fill it, a thin man with oblong steel-framed glasses resting uneasily on a thin bridged nose. A gray man.

Heath looked unchanged. The years had not further shriveled his shrunken body and he might be wearing the same pepper-and-salt suit. He was aware of Bart coming in from the heat of the street, pausing to let his eyes adjust to the dimmer room, moving then past the tellers, back to the rear desk.

Heath stood up, his pale parchment face looking too stiff to change expression. He offered a hand, a dry talon so fragile in its bone structure that it would crush easily. Layton watched his grip. He barely touched Heath's palm.

The banker indicated the chair beside the desk, a birdlike motion of his small head, and sank back into the wide, leather upholstered arms of Ryan Layton's throne. Like a child in the grip of a bear.

"I heard about last night." The voice was a whisper of breeze through reeds, indecisive. "Has the sheriff discovered anything?"

"He knows the man I shot. That's all."

"A bad homecoming. I wonder what they wanted." The light eyes behind the flat panes of the glasses were sharp.

Layton had never known Heath well. He had been the cashier, a shadow around the bank for as far back as Layton could remember. He shrugged.

"First, about my grandfather. I've heard rumors. I want the truth."

The small man shrunk further into the chair's embrace. "It is a tragedy, believe me. I don't like to think about it. Ryan Layton took me when I was young, made a place for me here at the bank. He taught me everything I know." He paused, his tongue touched his thin lips nervously. They looked blue in the weak light, as if he had not enough blood. "I don't like to talk about it even now. Oh, Ryan could be difficult at times, but I understood him. I didn't take his tantrums seriously; I knew they'd pass as quickly as they came." He peered sharply again at the captain. "As a boy you did not realize that about him."

Layton nodded unwillingly. It was true. He had had little self-discipline. It was true that he still had little. He would have to watch himself. He watched the banker.

"Was it in character that he'd try to kill a woman? Was it right for the court to commit him?"

"Judge Anders thought so, yes. Your grandfather's oldest friend. He broke down that night, right after he had signed the order. He cried. At the Palace Bar."

The banker looked as though he might weep himself. Layton brought him back to the present.

"So who's running the bank now, the mine, the other businesses?"

Heath's hands moved nervously, like two small white rabbits hunting a place to hide. "The Gabriel was put under a trusteeship by the court. The businesses were sold. The bank was sold to stockholders. I am running it, under their direction."

"So the mine is all that's left? Who are the trustees?"

"Your two cousins and Caleb Hewmark. You remember him?"

"Yes. Which means that Hewmark is running it. Neither Clint nor Dick ever had sense enough to breathe in and out alone."

Heath pressed his lips together as if to assure his making no comment. When he volunteered nothing more, Layton had to ask.

"Where does that leave me? Did the judge cut me out of the picture?"

The banker showed genuine shock. "Of course not. The trust is divided four ways."

"Someone might have bothered to tell me."

"But I wrote . . . I didn't know where you were, all we heard was a rumor that you had joined the army. I wrote to Washington, asking them to forward the message. I supposed that was why you came home."

Layton smiled in spite of himself. He wondered what Heath's reaction would be if he told the banker he was here because he had lost his temper and knocked down a superior officer.

"I never got it. It's probably lost on some clerk's desk in the War Department. I guess I'd better talk to Jack Priest." Priest had been his grandfather's lawyer.

"Jack's been dead for five years."

Layton stared at him. "Then who?"

"I think you'd better talk to Hewmark. He keeps an office at the mill."

"You mean he spends all his time here?"

"Well, he still has an office in Denver, but he's here most of the time. He's been trying to increase the mine's production. The returns haven't been as good as they used to be."

CHAPTER FIVE

The house his grandfather had built when the mine really began to pay was bigger than any of its neighbors. It stood on a small flat shelf, looking across the canyon at the mill, in the center of a hard packed yard enclosed in a picket fence.

From the main street a curving path wound up between other houses, climbing at a sharp incline to the shelf. The house had been painted white, not recently. The two climbing roses that had been his grandmother's pride now hid the trellises at either end of the narrow, roofed porch.

Layton climbed the path and memory climbed with him. It had been a dreaded trip in his boyhood, for usually he was being sent there to face Ryan's anger at some infraction of rules. His uncle's wife had early turned the disciplining of him over to the older Layton, and the hillside was closely associated with unpleasantness.

He stepped on the porch with no lift of home-coming, twisted the handle of the door bell. For a few minutes there was no sound within and he had almost concluded there was no one there when the door rattled and was pulled open. He found himself looking at a girl. She was tall, nearly as high as his shoulder. Her hair was fair and naturally curling, fluffing about her face. The eyes were gray and there was a line to her chin that might mean determination, even stubbornness.

She gave him a long, silent scrutiny that continued after he had taken off the weathered campaign hat. She looked from the crisp blond hair to the soft leather boots. Then she spoke in a voice that surprised him with its soft music.

"You must be Bart Layton."

He was puzzled that she knew who he was, or that he was in town. She saw his look and smiled quickly, a warming smile that transformed her face, making it beautiful.

"Don't be surprised. Clint told me you had come home. He was very glad."

"That," he said, "doesn't sound like my cousin."

Her laugh came. "Oh, I know. Your grandfather told me a great deal about you, how you and the boys never got along, how you went away and joined the army. He didn't like that. You were in the wrong army."

"The Civil War's been over twenty years."

"But he never accepted it. He felt the Southerners shouldn't have bowed. We used to argue sometimes. . . . But come in, why do I keep you standing out here? Because I'm so eager to talk to someone, I suppose. Not many bother to climb way up here."

He followed her into the old living room. It looked as he recalled it, the chairs with cowhide seats, the deep throated fireplace. It startled him to find the head of the deer he had shot when he was twelve still mounted above the mantel.

She studied him again. "You're not glad to be home?"

"Should I be? I came up to ask what happened to my grandfather."

All the humor went out of her face. "It was rather terrible. He'd been so good to me, helping me get the place teaching at the school . . . he was head of the school board."

"He would be." Ryan Layton had always had to be the head of everything, even a school district.

She ignored the comment. "And then he was hurt. Clint and Dick didn't know what to do about him. They asked me to come and look after him. I'd done some practical nursing back home."

Layton's eyes held on her, drawn to her. Women had aways attracted him, and in most of the posts where he had served they were few, only the wives of other officers. An enlisted man could find comfort with the saloon girls, an officer could

41

not. There were some disadvantages to having a commission.

His voice was flat. "They tell me he's crazy."

She made a gesture that would repulse the word. "He was queer after the accident, yes . . . but I didn't think he'd lost his mind, not until the morning he attacked me."

"You didn't have any warning?"

She hesitated. "Well . . . I suppose so. He developed a persecution complex. He thought people were trying to rob him, even kill him. I didn't take it seriously; a lot of people get that way as they get older."

"But why you? The one who was trying to help him?"

Her smile came again, more pained than humorous. "He got the idea I'd been sent up here to spy on him."

"By whom?"

"By your cousins. He thought they were stealing the mine from him. He thought because Clint had asked me to come here there was something between Clint and me."

Bart Layton was blunt. "Was there?"

Laughter ran through her, high and spontaneous. "How long since you've seen Clint?"

"Last night."

Her eyes opened wider. "And you can still ask . . . do you really think I could find such a—find him attractive?"

"No." His face clouded, but he could not dissemble. "Excuse me, but I've known women to do the damnedest things where a lot of money was concerned. I've been away a long time and this whole situation has got me confused."

She was standing before him, looking up into his face. Impulsively her hand came out to rest on his arm. "I understand. I won't take that as an insult." The gray eyes changed, deepening into blue. "It must be very hard, to come home after all this time and find no one in your family who cares, not many friends left."

He did not answer. Her quick sympathy embarrassed him. There had been few friends throughout his lonely life to care what happened to him. Not many in the army, no one really except Dugan. And Dugan was dead.

"What are you going to do?"

He said, "Find out about the mine, I guess. I understand that I'm a quarter owner."

"I hope it works out for you. I know mighty little about things like that, but from the gossip I judge it isn't doing so well."

"Thank you."

"I suppose you won't want me staying here at the house? I asked Dick and Clint, but neither wanted it. They told me to stay until it was sold."

His smile twisted. "I wouldn't know how to behave in a house. A hotel room is more my style."

"You're kind," she said.

"Apparently you were kind to my grandfather. We owe you something."

"Anyway," she changed the subject, "come up and have dinner. The food at the hotel isn't too much. Come tonight."

"Not tonight. I still have things to do today."

"Tomorrow night then."

He promised. He went back down the path, taking away a different feeling than he ever had before. He had never met a woman quite like this.

CHAPTER SIX

The mill had been built below the town, beside a small dam that blocked Montrose Creek into a pond. The ore carts arrived there from the mine, pulling up a twisting grade to dump their loads into the ore chutes. The broken rock then slid down into the crushers, on across the screens into the grinders where it was pulverized into fine dust. Thence it was fed into cyanide tanks to be leached and then floated to the top by pine oil while the sludge was carried away to the dump below. Like so many Colorado ores, the ore from the Gabriel was not free milling, but a highly complex telluride. The extraction was slow and expensive.

The noise in the mill was enormous. First the

thunder of the ten-ton stamps breaking up the boulders, next the scream of the jaw crushers cracking the pieces further, finally the pounding bounce of the ball mills. The whole building shook and filled with a fine dust which, held in suspension in the air, clogged the nostrils, stung the eyes, peppered clothes with a gritty coat.

Even in the office, removed as far from the stamps as possible, conversation was still difficult. Bart Layton found himself shouting to make himself heard. There were three to make hear: Dick and Clint Layton, his cousins, and Caleb Hewmark.

It was on Hewmark that he turned his attention. Hewmark was about forty, a blocky, powerfully built man, with a heavy yet still handsome face, a shock of dark hair now touched with gray against the scalp, and a ready, hearty voice that told he had found few enemies throughout the world. He had started in the mines as a boy, as a mucker. Luck, ability and driving will had pushed him up the business ladder. The rumor now was that the syndicate of which he was a part held substantial interests in mines from California all across the west.

Bart remembered him vaguely from his own childhood, a friend of his grandfather's, a young man in whom Ryan Layton had taken an interest, a man who laughed easily. That was what Bart remembered about him, how easily he laughed.

45

Hewmark was saying now in a voice trained to carry through the racket, "It's good to have you back. I just wish the news was better, about conditions, for you to come home to." He pulled some sheets from the littered desk and passed them across. "But you can see what we're up against. In the first six months of this year the company has lost almost a hundred thousand dollars. It doesn't take a prophet to know we can't go on like this forever."

Layton did not comprehend the list of figures. Even in his own mind he made no pretense of understanding business. He had no experience in this department, although he was familiar with the working of the mine, the mill, from his early days of hanging around them. He hardly looked at the sheets.

"What's your program? You're a practical miner and none of the rest of us are."

In spite of the easy smile on Hewmark's lips Layton found the eyes hard, watchful, even remote.

"Good question." Hewmark took his time, apparently thinking about each word with care. "The Gabriel is suffering from the same blight that affects many mines which have been worked for years. The shafts and laterals go deeper and deeper. Every hundred feet we go down makes it cost more to raise the ore, and the water keeps increasing. A lot of our equipment is old, obsolete.

We put in new pumps last fall and already they're inadequate. And the value of the ore we mill decreases constantly. It's a case of diminishing returns."

"So what are you doing?"

"I loaned the company a quarter of a million dollars to make up the deficits, install the new pumps, replace some of the ball mills. That money is nearly gone. We've less than a hundred thousand in working capital left. When that runs out I doubt we can raise any more. My syndicate surely won't furnish it and I doubt that anyone else will."

"What do we do?"

"One of two things. Hang on until we can't meet the payroll and have to close, or find some outside buyer."

The question seemed obvious to Layton. "If we're in such poor shape why should anyone want to buy?"

Hewmark spread his hands, laughing a little as if he enjoyed some private joke. "Mining is a gambler's business. A lot of men in it know as much about the Gabriel as we do, possibly more. They also know we're undercapitalized. Somebody among them will figure that if he can step in here with enough backing to modernize, cut costs, open up new ore bodies, he might make it into a paying operation. And there's always the dream of another bonanza maybe ten feet further down . . .

but there's the greater likelihood of bankruptcy, which we're in no position to risk."

Layton watched him closely, his eyes hooded by half-closed lids. He was reminded of conferences he had sat in with Apache leaders, each side weighing the other, trying to seek out weakness.

"Have you somebody in mind who might be interested?"

Hewmark moved his handsome head from side to side. "I haven't, not offhand. Up until a couple of months ago I thought we could pull out by ourselves. I don't think so now. If you say so I'll start making inquiries around Denver, let the word get out that we might sell if we got the right offer."

Layton felt oddly dissatisfied, largely because he knew so little of what Hewmark was talking about. It was a disadvantage he did not like. His uncertainty was in his voice.

"Let me think about it. I've only been back a day and this is all new to me." He looked to his cousins. "Walk along with me? I want to talk about the old man."

Dick stood up, obviously glad to be leaving. He was a thinner version of Clint, with the same indecisiveness in his expression.

Outside, they turned up-canyon toward the town proper, the noise of the mill following, muting slowly. Bart Layton rubbed his ears.

"If I had to work in that clatter all the time I'd

lose my mind. Maybe that's what happened to Ryan."

Dick Layton sounded positive. "No, it was the beam. It hit his head. I think a bone is pressing on his brain."

Bart had another thought that he wanted to bring up. "You married, Dick?"

His cousin looked at him in surprise. "My wife died last year. I keep forgetting you've been away."

"What do you think of Mary Dorne?"

Both of them looked at him then. "Think of her?"

"She's an attractive woman, very. Has she ever been married?"

The cousins exchanged glances. Dick answered. It was usually Dick who took the lead. "Not that I know of."

"Ever been mixed up with a man, here in Montrose?"

Again they exchanged glances; again Dick shook his head. "Never heard of any."

"Was she setting her cap for Grandpaw?"

Dick laughed loudly, an empty sound. "Are you crazy? He's seventy years old."

"And has a lot of money."

"Not now. You heard Hewmark."

Bart's tone was bleak. "I heard him."

Dick stepped out of the way of a freight wagon and turned around. "Meaning you don't believe him?"

"I don't know anything about it. But all the time I was growing up I thought of the old man as the richest miner in the country. It takes a little getting used to, thinking about him being broke."

Dick sounded fatalistic. "It's true. We've even got the house up for sale. It costs money to keep him in that Bedford place. It isn't publicly owned, you know."

Layton had not thought about that.

Clint cut in. "I only hope we can find a buyer for the mine before we have to close it. If it closes I don't know what Dick and I will do."

That was something Bart did understand. Neither man had ever made a living. Both were a good deal older than he, had been in their early thirties when he left, and even then they were showing weaknesses. Clint had always liked the bottle and Bart had helped put him to bed more than once. Dick had been a gambler, a poor one, supporting the poker tables at the Palace since Bart could remember. He guessed they had not changed. The mark of alcohol was plain in Clint's flabby, veined cheeks and puffed eyes, and Dick's face held a furtive nervousness. Bart started to turn away as they reached the courthouse, then he stopped, turned to Clint.

"Last night after I talked to you, where did you go?"

The fat man looked startled. "Go? What makes you think I went anywhere?"

"You weren't in your room when the shooting started."

"Oh." Clint seemed to pull himself together with a visible effort. "I went to tell Dick you'd come home. I thought he ought to know."

Layton could not tell whether he was lying. He left them, went on up the boardwalk and in through the main entrance of the courthouse.

The building had been the pride of Montrose when he was a boy, the largest structure in town. Wooden built, two stories, it stood on the canyon side opposite the mill, the first floor given over to the tax man, the county treasurer, the sheriff's office and the jail. Above were the courtroom, district attorney's office and the judge's chambers.

He climbed. His steps echoed ahead on the dusty, hollow treads. Except for the pervading drum of the stamps half a mile away, the halls were silent. The rhythm of the stamps was the heartbeat of Montrose. When they fell silent Montrose would die.

The courtroom was empty. The district attorney's office, seen through the partly open door, was deserted. Bart Layton was almost surprised to find Judge Anders at his desk.

Frail, white-haired, his thin face marked by deep lines, his piercing dark eyes recessed into a face that had no more meat than a death's head, Anders watched his door as the footsteps came toward it and the visitor came through. Then he stood up.

"Bart. Bart Layton."

Layton went in toward the rolltop desk. "Judge. It's good to see you."

Anders extended a long blue-veined hand. Layton took it and Anders closed his other over it.

"Sit down, boy. I heard from Fred Foster that you were back."

Bart Layton settled into the chair and watched the judge sit down. "I came to ask you about my grandfather."

"I thought you had." A spasm of what might have been pain crossed the old face, clouded the deep-set eyes. "There wasn't a damned thing I could do but commit him, Bart. It was as hard a job as I ever had in my life."

"Clint tells me nobody can see him."

Judge Anders sighed. "That's the rule. Bedford is a private institution. We have no place for such cases in the county, so we have an arrangement with them. The family pays what it's able, the county takes care of the rest."

"But I want to see him."

The judge spread his transparent hands. "There's nothing much I can do about it. If you want to take him out, move him down to Denver, say, you'll have to go through an action to have the commitment set aside. Frankly, as a friend, I'd advise against it. He has a deep persecution complex, made some absurd charges at the hearing. Bart, he just is no longer rational."

"What if I talk to the people at Bedford? Who's the doctor?"

"A man named Thorpe. It won't do any good, it's the rule of the place. I'd forget it if I were you. It would bring you no pleasure to see him and would probably give him a bad time too."

Layton put the question aside, thinking rapidly. Then he said, "What about this trust you set up? Am I a member?"

"Of course. You share equally in a vote with your cousins and Hewmark."

"What do you think of Hewmark?"

The judge hesitated. "He's a shrewd man and he stands to lose a great deal of money if the mine closes. And he is not the kind of man who likes to lose money."

"Is anyone?"

"No, I suppose not." The old man sounded tired. "I've been in this town almost since your grandfather opened the Gabriel. Montrose has been my home; I've been proud of it. I've seen other camps fold up and I hate to see Montrose go that way. I don't expect you to share my feeling. After all, you didn't have a particularly happy life here."

Bart Layton left him to reverie and descended the stairs, turned along the lower hall to the sheriff's office.

Fred Foster was there, alone in the outer room that was separated from the single jail cell by a grilled door. The cell was empty.

"Nothing new." He motioned Layton to a seat and shoved forward a half-filled box of cigars. "I take it the rest of your night wasn't disturbed?"

Layton took a cigar and used the lighting of it as a pause to think. Foster had been as near a friend as he had had here, but he realized that he still did not fully trust him. He thought, *What's the matter with me?* Dugan's death had bitten deep. He knew that the bullet had been intended for him, that the sergeant's death had not been intended. He did not know who wanted him dead, or why, but he was beginning to have an idea. He said to Foster,

"Have you heard anything about high-grading at the mine?"

Foster looked at him through the rising cigar smoke, squinting a little as if the smoke disturbed his eyes.

"There'll always be talk of high-grading as long as there's ore in the ground. Got anything specific in mind?"

Layton shrugged. "Nothing specific. I understand my grandfather suggested it at the sanity hearing."

"Your grandfather was—is a sick man." Foster's tone was flat. "Bart. I'm your friend, right?"

Layton nodded slowly. In the old days Foster would never have put their relationship into words.

"All right. I don't know what this is all about.

Maybe those bums in the bar spotted you, didn't know you, and trailed you to the hotel figuring you were a stranger in town and safe to rob."

"Believe that?"

After a long moment Foster let his eyes fall. "I don't know. I honestly don't know. But if that isn't the case, what is?"

"Somebody doesn't want me in Montrose."

"Why?"

"That's what I don't know. But it has to have something to do with the mine."

"You mean you're buying the high-grading story?"

"Perhaps."

"Look." Foster bent across the desk, very earnest. "We don't have high-grading around here for one very simple reason. The ore is not free milling. You can't just break up the quartz and pick out the gold. Either with your fingers or mercury. It has to be treated, cyanided. Supposing a miner or someone else stole a ton of ore. He'd have to take it to some mill. And the only mill in the canyon belongs to the Gabriel. Right?"

"He might haul it out on mule back."

Foster barked a laugh. "Where to? It's fifty miles to the next nearest mill. Even if he got that far without somebody checking up, there'd be questions wherever he took it. The Gabriel's ore is well known, easy to identify."

Layton had no answer.

"Look," said Foster. It seemed to be his favorite word. "It's none of my business, but I've heard rumors that Hewmark is trying to find a buyer. If he does, for your own sake help him. Get out of a losing deal."

Layton said bluntly, "Why are you so interested?"

A dull flush came up under Foster's heavy tan. For a moment he opened his mouth as if with a sharp retort. Then he quieted.

"I'm not interested. Not in you, not in the mine as such. I'm interested in the town. I've never been away, not like you have. I stayed here. I took a job as a stinking deputy, at eighty dollars a month. I held it until the sheriff died and then ran for the place. I've got a wife and two kids and a comfortable home. And I want to keep it. That answer your question?"

"Not entirely."

"It should. If an outfit moves in here that's big enough, with enough money to spend on new equipment, on deepening the shafts and running levels, Montrose will survive. If they don't, Montrose is finished. That's all there is to it."

CHAPTER SEVEN

Coming out of the dimness of the courthouse hall the brilliance of the sun blinded him. He stopped to wait for his sight to clear, but he was not yet fully adjusted as he moved down the short walk toward the street.

The girl was small. At first he was not certain it was a girl. Her black hair was cut short, a mass which the steady downdraft from the canyon above blew around her face. She wore a boy's shirt, white, and faded coveralls. Both were very clean.

He side-stepped to give her passage. She side-stepped with him. They were like dancers in a "square" following a caller. He moved the other way. She moved with him, blocking his path. He smiled apologetically. She said without smiling,

"I want to talk to you."

Not until she spoke was he certain that she was a girl. Her face was too thin, too intent. Only the eyes gave a hint of feminine beauty.

"All right. What would you like to talk about?"

"Montrose."

He looked across her head toward the lackluster street. "And just why do you want to?"

"Because you're Bart Layton. Because you only just came back, and maybe you can see your

57

nose in front of your face, and maybe you can do something to save the mine and this town."

He blinked at her. "Who are you?"

She flicked a hand as if her identity was of small importance. "Sarah Hobart."

"And how do you know I'm Bart Layton?"

"Everybody knows who you are. Everybody's watching to see what you'll do." Her tone said that he was being stupid.

"Meaning?"

"Can't you see? It's dying." There was feeling in her voice as if she were talking about a beloved relative. "It's dying, and everything that people have made here will die with it. It isn't the first town I've seen die."

He looked at her with growing curiosity. It was hard to guess her age. "How old are you?"

The dark eyes flashed for an instant, then she said, "Eighteen."

"How long have you been in Montrose?"

"Five years."

"Before that?"

"California. Idaho. Virginia City."

"You move around a lot."

"My father's a miner. We go where the work is."

He was beginning to get the idea. "And if the mine closes here there will be no work."

She bobbed her dark head. "I'm glad you can see that. We've bought a house here. Everything we've got is in that house. If the mine closes we'll have to leave, and no one will want the house. We'll leave with nothing. And we aren't the only ones. Hundreds of people are in the same trap."

He looked again at the town below them, the straggling cluster of houses, each representing a family which in one or another form drew its living from the mine.

He had never before actually thought about things from this angle. He had been thinking of the mine as a property that belonged to him, to his cousins and, yes, to Caleb Hewmark. He remembered what Foster had just said. And he began to have an inkling of the fear that gripped the people of this town.

Aloud he said, "If the mine can't make money, there's nothing to pay miners with. It can't keep going."

"It doesn't make money because it's being stolen blind."

He looked at her sharply. "Ever since I got home there have been hints about high-grading all around me. Everybody whispers about it. But nobody tells me when or how it's done. Are you just spreading gossip or do you really know something?"

Her small chin set stubbornly. "My father has been a miner for thirty years. He knows mines. He knows ore. He's a shift foreman, and he knows that the ore dug out on his level is extremely rich."

"Where is he now? At the mine?"

"At home. A rock fell on his foot last week. He can't go back to work until tomorrow."

"Let's go talk to him."

Her eyes searched Layton's face for a full moment as if she measured him. Then without a word she turned and paced along the walk.

The house was small, a frame affair of probably four rooms, but the outside was in good repair, neatly kept, and a small bed of flowers bloomed in the baked front yard.

The man on the porch was big. His shoulders were massive, his hands work worn but powerful, looking strangely uncomfortable folded in his lap. His right foot was propped on a box, swathed in bandage. He watched them come along the path and turn in across the yard. The father's heavy face creased in a frown of displeasure as the daughter brought the visitor to the bottom of the two steps and said,

"This is Captain Bart Layton. He wants to talk to you. This is my father. His name is Tom."

Tom Hobart did not smile. He did not speak. Layton hesitated, sensing hostility, not understanding it. He said finally, "Your daughter tells me you can give me some information about the mine."

Hobart spat into the dust of the yard. "You had no right to ask her. You shouldn't have spoke to her."

Sarah Hobart's voice was tart. "He did not ask

me and he did not speak to me first. I spoke to him."

The miner's displeasure hardened to a sullen anger. "I told you to keep out of this."

"You told me." Her voice that had been soft and warm raised in shrillness. "You men, grumble, grumble among yourselves and never do a thing."

"It's not our business."

Layton guessed that this was an old argument between them.

The girl went on, waspish. "If it isn't your business, whose is it?"

"Daughter." The tone was a roar and Layton guessed that only the injured foot kept the man from lunging out of his chair, shaking the girl. "A man learns what-for when he first goes underground. You keep quiet about the mine you work for. You do not talk about it, not to anybody outside it. You do not say a word about what kind of ore is being dug."

"Captain Layton is one of the owners."

The heavy lids lowered, the smoking eyes nearly closed. "Then it is his business to learn what-for for himself."

He took his bandaged foot off the box, lowered it gently, stood up, pressing his big hands down on the chair arms, lifting himself upright. He twisted on his good foot, hopped to the screen door and disappeared inside.

Layton and the girl looked at each other in

silence. Then she said in a small tone, a choke in her voice, "I'm sorry. I shouldn't have bothered you. I guess I was wrong."

He didn't believe this. He felt suddenly very sorry for her. He did not know exactly what had happened, but her shoulders that had been so straight now drooped. Life seemed to have gone out of her voice.

"I understand," he said, but he did not understand. "Did you know my grandfather?"

"Everyone knew him. He saved my father's life."

"Did you think he was crazy?"

She moved her shoulders. "That's what they said, what everyone said."

"But you?"

"I don't know."

Suddenly, startling him, she jumped the stairs, onto the porch, raced across it and flung into the house, the screen slamming behind her.

Layton stood motionless, held by surprise. He resisted the impulse to go after her. After a little he turned away, back along the curving path, uncertain and disturbed.

Behind the front window curtain Sarah Hobart watched him go, willing him to come back, a sob catching in her throat. Her father came from the kitchen, pushing a chair as a makeshift crutch. He was still angry.

"What the hell made you bring that young squirt here?"

"He isn't a squirt and he isn't so young. He does own part of the mine."

"What does he know about mines? He's as much a fool as those idiot cousins. I've told you and told you, Caleb Hewmark is the only one knows what he's doing."

"I don't like him. I don't like a thief."

"You don't know that he is."

"I know what I think."

He said savagely, "You didn't say that to young Layton?"

She shook her head.

"Don't. If the Gabriel is ever to pay again, Hewmark has to be the one to make it so. If he ever found out we were working against him I'd never go underground again."

She faced him, unable to keep the contempt out of her young eyes. Once she had thought him the wisest, the best man in the world. But life had not been kind to Tom Hobart. Someplace along the way, perhaps her mother's death, had taken the heart and the will to fight out of him. She walked out of the room, out of the house. She wanted to go away and hide. She did not know where to go.

CHAPTER EIGHT

Bart Layton rode with a quirk on his lips, thinking back on his meeting with the Hobart girl. She was so intense, so determined. It pleased him to compare her with one of the mountain chipmunks darting among the timber and rocks. His horse had pushed forward steadily all afternoon, but at nightfall he was still some ten miles from Bedford.

He pulled up at a small mountain stream that boiled down the steep slope and crossed the trail beneath a pole bridge. He built a tiny fire there, heated coffee and ate the two sandwiches he had stuffed into his saddle bags. After that rest he mounted and went on in the gathering darkness.

He did not know exactly how he could manage it, but he fully intended to talk to his grandfather. The resolve had come as he had walked away from Sarah Hobart's house, for it had seemed obvious he would get small satisfaction from anyone in Montrose.

Bedford was a much smaller community than Montrose, a hill town that had been the county seat until Ryan Layton opened his mine and pulled the business to the canyon. With the business had gone the courthouse, and now little remained to give Bedford a reason for living.

There was the hospital. That was what Thorpe called his establishment. It was a long wooden building surrounded by a high pole stockade, looking to Layton more like a prison or fort. It had, in fact, once been an army post. The main gate was closed, locked on the inside. Through it few lights glowed from the main building. There was no other break in the fence. He rode around it through the darkness of near midnight.

By standing in the saddle, he thought, he could easily climb over. He did not know how tightly it was guarded, but probably they would not be too alert. They would be more interested in keeping the inmates from escaping than preventing someone outside from breaking in.

He put the horse into the shadow, close against the corner, and tied it to one of the upright logs. He caught hold of the sharpened top of the log, lifted himself up the rough wall until he could throw one leg over the barrier. He held there, resting, catching his breath, looking down inside. The big building squatted in the center of a trampled exercise ground. The gate was to his right some fifty feet, a small guardhouse beside it.

In the main building a light burned behind a center door that probably opened on a reception room, but there was no sign of anyone about. He brought his other leg over and dropped the ten feet to the hard ground; then, keeping in the shadow, he moved to the guardhouse.

It was small, about five feet square. The open door showed him lantern light and a man sitting in a chair tipped back against the wall, his eyes closed.

Layton drew his gun, moved into the bright doorway and stood so that the gun showed clearly in the lantern light.

"Wake up."

The guard was a burly man. He filled the chair. His eyes flicked open, staring without comprehension for a full minute at the man before him, his mind fighting sleep. Then he jerked alert, the forelegs of the chair slamming to the floor.

"Who the hell are you?"

"Just don't make any noise."

The man looked at the heavy gun. His mouth opened to protest, then it closed without a sound coming out.

Layton said, "Show me where Ryan Layton is."

The man's mouth opened again, framing a denial, then again closed, but he shrugged.

"Show me."

The guard's voice came. "Mister, nobody sees him. That's orders straight from Thorpe himself. It's worth my job."

"It's worth your life if you don't."

The guard believed him. He heaved his bulk out of the chair with a sigh. He wore a gun in the holster at his hip. Layton lifted it from the leather and tossed it across the yard.

"All right, let's go."

"If they catch you it will be rough. I don't know what your game is, but—"

"Don't worry about it. I'll be right behind you. If you start anything you'll get yourself hurt."

The guard debated with himself but did not answer. He crossed the compound and opened the main door. The reception room was empty, echoing as they moved on to the door in the west wall. That door gave on a long corridor, where a bracket lamp turned half way down burned against the wall.

There was no one in sight, no sound. The guard led Layton past doors marked Doctor Thorpe, Dispensary, Receiving, and paused at the end of the hall before an unlabeled door. It was a heavier panel with a window, grilled with iron bars. The guard jerked his head toward it.

Layton said, "Open it."

Again the guard hesitated in protest, then with a heavy shrug he pulled a fist full of keys from a pocket, chose one, thrust it in the lock and shoved the panel open.

From the darkness a quavering voice came at them. "What is it? What's going on?"

Layton said to the guard, "If there's a lamp, light it."

The man moved past him to the side wall, lifted the chimney from the wall fixture and lighted the wick. The flaring flame showed a small room, a single high window, a wash stand and dresser and a single bed. In one corner stood a wheelchair with straps dangling from the arms.

Ryan Layton lay on the bed, a harness around his shoulders holding him down. His black eyes glittered hotly, reflecting the flame, squinting as they adjusted to the new brightness. The voice was petulant, harsh.

"What you want in here now?"

The guard had turned, watching with hard, calculating eyes. Bart Layton read the look.

"I wouldn't advise you to start anything."

The man spread his hands, a negative gesture denying any such intention. Layton did not believe him.

"Go on over and sit in the wheelchair."

The man did not like it, but when Bart lifted the nose of his gun he moved, reluctantly, and sat down.

"Turn it around."

The man swung the chair to face the wall and Layton crossed quickly, fastening the straps around the guard's wrists. The guard was silent, his shoulders rigid with anger. Layton turned back to the bed, studying the old man strapped against the mattress, the bright eyes now taking in every movement in the room.

Bart Layton was shocked at what he saw. The eyes were shrunken into the skull, the cheeks were gray, the lips held a blue tinge. But the voice for all its quaver was strong.

"What in the hell is going on?"

Layton said, "Do you know me, Ryan?"

"Damn it, of course I know you. You think I'm crazy, I wouldn't know you?" The words had an ominous suggestion in the white room. The old man did not miss it. He added, "Sure you do, sure. At least, you'd like to think I've lost my mind, just like the others."

Bart Layton had come to stand above the bed, unconscious that he still held his gun in his hand.

"What others?"

The quaver intensified with the old man's deep feeling. "What others? What others? Don't you come mealy-mouthing around me, boy. You know what others. That damn Hewmark. That damned grabbing, two-timing woman he's sleeping with. Dick. Clint. All of them got their heads together and fixed to get me locked up in here. She's been telling the town, whispering around that I was going nuts ever since I got hurt. Now the whole place thinks I'm loco."

"Why would they do that?"

"You don't know . . . go ask them." Ryan sounded like a peevish child. He was, Bart realized, somewhat senile. But certainly he did not sound crazy.

Layton schooled himself to patience, using the tone he would have used with a child. "I came over to ask you direct, to hear what you yourself had to say. I just got home."

"Come back to help steal the mine."

"From what I hear around town the mine is no longer worth the stealing."

The old man's eyes burned with a new rage. "Lies, lies, lies. The Gabriel's richer than she ever was. Why else would they be trying to do me out of it? Can't you savvy plain English? After I got hurt and couldn't get down to the mill, Caleb Hewmark and that woman cooked up the whole scheme. They had a free hand. I couldn't move by myself, had to send all the orders to the men by Mary Dorne. I trusted her—and she crossed me up. She ordered whatever Hewmark wanted ordered."

"How did they work it?"

The grandfather looked as if he thought his grandchild was the weak-minded one. "Don't ask fool questions. They stole the gold. That's what I'm telling you. The mine is producing more than it ever did."

Bart Layton was not convinced. It was perfectly natural for an old man to want to believe that nothing ever changed. Nor was it hard to imagine that Ryan would believe he was being robbed. Old people often developed persecution complexes, but there was not much point in arguing. "Just what makes you so certain?"

Ryan flushed, his words choking on his impatience. "They said it right out. I heard them, Mary and that thief that I helped get started in the business. They thought I was asleep. He come up to the house, they were out on the porch, laughing about how smart they were, how they'd stolen gold from the mine and used it to loan me a quarter of a million dollars, for which Hewmark took a quarter interest in the Gabriel. He told her they would keep stealing and loaning the money back until they took over the whole mine. That's when I saw red. I knew I couldn't fight them both, not from that damned chair. I wheeled into the kitchen and got the knife. If I'd had a gun I'd have shot them. I waited until Hewmark left, then I called the woman. She didn't deny it. She said there was nothing I could do, that no one would believe me no matter what I said. So, I tried to kill her."

There was no sign of insanity in any of it to Bart Layton. Given Ryan's famous temper, that was exactly what he would have done. Crippled, entirely at the mercy of the woman and her lover, he would strike in the only way left open to him. He had had no one to turn to for help. Both Dick and Clint were powerless against anyone with a brain. The only part that bothered Bart was the high-grading itself. How could it be done with a complex ore?

He came to his decision abruptly. "All right, Ryan. I'm taking you home."

The old man shook his head. Suddenly all the fight seemed to drain out of him. He squeezed his eyes tight shut, but not tight enough to keep a tear from forcing out between the thin lids.

"They won't let you. They don't dare let me go . . . never, never, never."

Bart Layton had never expected to feel sorry for this man, this tyrant who had browbeaten everyone with whom he came in contact. Once he would have gloried in the humbling of this one who had made his boyhood a daily hell. But now it was with deep hurt that he looked at the mine owner, strapped to the bed like some foaming, vicious animal.

"I'll take you out." He said it between his clamped teeth.

The eyes opened. They reached up, searching to read hope in the craggy face above. The lips formed a word, little more than a whisper. "When?"

Layton hesitated, needing a plan. It was obvious that he could not take the invalid away on a horse. He would have to get a buckboard and arrange a bed in the rear. Yet he did not want to leave the old man in this place any longer than was barely necessary.

"I'll be back for you as soon as possible."

The face closed in again, plainly showing that Ryan had no trust in him, that he thought he was again being deserted. Layton did not insist. He prodded the guard into the hallway, saying, "Where do I find Doctor Thorpe?"

The man threw him a muddy look. "He's asleep."

"I didn't ask that. Where is he?"

"In his room, I guess. Unless he's visiting with one of the nurses." Discolored teeth showed in a mocking grin.

"Show me."

"Now wait a minute, mister big. I didn't give you any trouble, but if I take you to the doc he'll fire me sure as I'm a foot high."

"And if you don't you'll have a cracked head. Take your choice."

The man eyed the heavy gun steady in Layton's hand. Again he shrugged. He turned and led the way back to the reception room and through it to another corridor which served the living quarters of the staff. He paused before a closed door and knocked. There was no answer, and he knocked again.

A sleepy voice came through to them. "What is it?"

"Richards. There's a man here wants to see you."

"Tell him to come back in the morning."

Layton shoved the guard aside and tried the door with his free hand. It was unlocked. He thrust it wide and motioned Richards ahead of him into the room.

"Light the lamp."

He stayed in the hallway, protected by the door jamb until the yellow glow showed him the interior.

The doctor was a big man, looking huge in his striped night shirt, his bullet head covered by a matching night cap. He was angry, hunching on the edge of the bed, braced on powerful, hairy legs. He glared at Layton, at the gun still hanging loosely in his right hand.

"What the hell do you think you're doing, busting in here like this? No one's allowed to come in after sundown. That's the rule."

"Whose rule?"

Thorpe's glare darkened on his unwanted guest. "Mine. This is a hospital. The people here need quiet and rest."

"Tied in their beds?"

Thorpe swelled explosively, then he mastered his fury enough to say coldly, "If they need restraint, yes. Some of them are very dangerous."

"Would you call Ryan Layton dangerous?"

"Extremely."

"A man confined to a wheelchair?"

Thorpe thrust his body upright, rigid as a tree trunk.

"For your information, whoever you are, he has tried twice to burn down this building."

Bart found himself wanting to smile. With Ryan's strong temper the old man could be another Samson, willing to destroy himself if in doing it he could destroy his prison.

"I am his grandson," he said. "And I am going to take him out of here. Whether or not you like it.

Tell your man here to get a buckboard and a team ready."

Thorpe's hard eyes bugged and again he fought for control. "Ryan Layton was committed here by the court and here he will stay until such time as the court chooses to rescind that order. Now, you have exactly two minutes to clear out of here."

"This says I'm taking my grandfather with me." Layton moved the gun. "I'm going to shoot you in the right leg, Doctor, and if that doesn't convince you that I mean what I'm saying I'll shoot you in the left one. Maybe I'll hit a kneecap. I'm fair with a gun. Did you ever see what a forty-five bullet will do to a knee?"

Thorpe stood stolid, silent. Layton pushed on.

"How much is Caleb Hewmark paying you to keep Ryan locked up?"

"I don't have to listen to your insults."

"But you have to tell Richards to get that buckboard." He glanced toward the silent guard. "And don't you get any clever ideas on your own. If anyone tries to stop me Doctor Thorpe gets a bullet, and that one not in the legs."

The guard glanced at the doctor. Thorpe said in a strangled voice, "Do as he says. I think he's crazier than the old man."

The guard started for the door, glad to be out of the room.

Layton said to Thorpe, "You'd better pull on

some pants unless you want to wander around the landscape in that shirt."

The big man looked at him without comprehension.

"You're going to take a ride, say about ten miles, just to make sure you don't send someone after us."

"You do know that you're breaking the law?"

"It's not the first time I've broken the rules." Layton was indifferent. "Get some pants and shoes on."

Without grace the man turned to the wardrobe and dressed. Layton prodded him out to the hall and to the reception room. They waited there a full five minutes before Richards appeared to say the buckboard was ready.

"Now," said Layton, "go get my grandfather. Bring him here."

Again the guard looked to Thorpe. The doctor merely nodded. Apparently the fight had seeped out of him.

When Richards came back, pushing the wheelchair, Ryan Layton was grinning, almost bouncing. He shook a bony finger at Thorpe cackling to Bart, "Shoot the bastard, boy. Gun him down for me."

"That won't help us."

"It'll make me feel good. If you're too squeamish to squeeze that trigger, gimme the gun."

"Never mind. We can worry about him later.

Right now the important thing is to get you away from here."

Ryan Layton made no gesture of hiding his disappointment. "Doc," he shook the finger again, "if you ever cross my path again I'll have a gun in my pocket, ready. Believe me, that's a promise."

Bart realized that Ryan was behaving more and more like a child, taking a child's pleasure in unrealistic threats. He said sharply to the guard, "Take him out and put him in the wagon."

The man no longer hesitated. He wheeled the chair through the door and down the ramp to the mud wagon waiting in the oblong of light. Layton waited until Ryan was lifted onto the tailgate, then motioned to the doctor with his gun.

"All right, let's go."

Over the doctor's head Layton saw how black the night had grown, the moon vanished behind a rising bank of cloud. He had the fleeting thought that they might get wet before they reached Montrose. Then Thorpe was through the door and Layton followed him.

He was barely clear of the entrance when a swinging club crashed down on the wrist of his gun hand with shattering force. The hand went numb. The heavy weapon fell from his nerveless fingers. And at the same moment a man he did not see came out of the dark on his other side. Arms wrapped around him and a husky voice shouted at his ear.

"Got him."

The man was trying to lift him from his feet.

The enclosure exploded into sound, shouts from the attackers, from the guard, yells of rage from Ryan Layton perched helplessly in the bed of the wagon. Thorpe was barking orders.

Pain was beginning to burn in the numbed arm, but Bart had no use of his fingers. He tripped the man who held him, and they dropped to the ground together, Layton on the bottom. The man who had swung the club circled cautiously, trying for a clear blow at Layton's head. In the uncertain light he missed twice. The third time Layton twisted, swinging the man he grappled with over, and the club snapped down on that one's shoulder.

A shout of pain, a string of curses boiled from him and his grip on Layton relaxed. Layton squirmed out from under, pivoted up to his knees. His fingers still would not work, but he was able to use the arm to help shove up to his feet.

He saw the man with the club in the oblong of light, charging forward, the club held in both hands, high above his head. Layton dived under it. He caught the man around the chest, hooked his heel behind the other's leg, sent him sprawling backward to the ground. Spinning, Layton found the first man struggling to pull a gun from a holster at his hip, saw Richards charging from the rear of the buckboard, saw Thorpe closing in.

He turned and ran, heading for the gate. Behind him a gun roared. The bullet tore at the shoulder of his coat. He reached the guardhouse beside the gate and jumped around the protection of its corner as the gun spoke again, hearing the bullet tear through the sun-dried boards. Then he tugged up the bar that held the gate closed, cracked the gate open and flung through.

Behind him the thud of running feet chased him, cries followed him and Thorpe's shouts rode over all.

"Head him off. Head him off. Don't let the bastard get away."

Against the bull voice came the eerie screech of his grandfather's urging. "Keep going, boy. Keep going. They ain't never licked a Layton yet."

He ran along the shadow of the stockade. Here it was so dark that he could not watch his footing. Three times he stumbled, nearly falling over obstructing brush. But the very gloom saved him. As the pursuers burst through the gate they milled uncertainly, peering around the dark, trying to decide which way he had gone.

He slowed, stopped. The idea of leaving Ryan Layton in this madhouse for another hour seared through him, but without a gun he stood no chance of doing anything else. It left him no choice but to get away, to keep alive and return to his mission later.

He reached his horse, freed the animal and

swung silently to the saddle. He walked it around the angle of the stockade, walked it another fifty feet, then he touched it with the spurs and plunged ahead through the night, turning back toward Montrose.

CHAPTER NINE

Caleb Hewmark was angry, fuming at the man who had just come into the mill, his voice barely carrying above the racket.

"McCall, what do you mean, coming here? I told you never to show yourself around here, didn't I?"

The guard from the asylum waited it out, then said with bland indifference, "Thorpe sent me. He thought you'd want to know that young Layton was at the hospital last night."

Hewmark was jolted. "Bart Layton?"

The man massaged his shoulder where the club had struck it. "Maybe that's his name. I didn't meet him socially."

"What was he doing there? What did he want?"

"To take his grandfather home, he said. And he tried to do just that."

"Did he talk to the old man?"

"Sure did, from what Richards said."

"Damn it. My orders were he wasn't to talk to anyone."

"I know, I know. The gate was locked. Who'd expect some wild monkey to climb over the wall? Anyhow, where's the harm done? He didn't get the old man away, he's still safe there."

Hewmark's quick mind went over this new situation and he nodded grudgingly.

"Yes, he's safe. Well . . . tell Thorpe to sit tight. And now you, get out of here before somebody comes in and sees you."

Impatiently he waited where he was, giving McCall time to reach his horse and ride off. Then he left the mill and climbed the path to the house that had been Ryan Layton's home.

He had not visited this place in the daytime since Ryan had been put away, not wanting the town to guess at the close relationship between himself and Mary Dorne, and when he went there at night he went with a sense of awe unnatural to him. It still amazed him that a woman like the ex-school teacher would become his mistress.

He had always been afraid of what he considered good women. All of his early lovemaking had been confined to the so-called saloon girls, and until Ryan Layton had had his accident he had barely spoken to Mary Dorne.

But after the accident, with the old man condemned to the wheelchair, it had been necessary that he go to the house to transact the mine business. And from the moment he saw her in this new environment, he wanted her.

He could not now remember who first suggested the possibility of their taking over the Gabriel. But it had been her imagination that had seen how they could buy the mine by stealing the price from the mine itself. And over the years they had taken two hundred and fifty thousand dollars, loaning the money back to the company for operating capital, taking a quarter interest in the stock as security.

This had given Hewmark a voice in the management, in fact the dominant voice. Neither Dick nor Clint had ever shown any interest in the operation beyond drawing out what funds they could. And his project had been to continue working at an apparent loss, until he could pilfer enough to buy out the brothers.

Bart Layton's untimely return played havoc with that picture. Now he would have to move fast. He would have to set up a phony syndicate in Denver and arrange to sell the mine to it.

He did not like the pressure this change put upon him, and his mood was sour as he left the mill. But as he climbed the hill, came up onto the porch, anticipation overwhelmed him. He was giddy with the rising elation he always experienced when he knew he was going to see the girl. The effect she had on him was tremendous. In any association with women he had always been the dominant one, and he was smart enough to see that in this case Mary Dorne was the stronger. He did not care. He wanted only to get possession of the mine, to end the subterfuge under which they lived. To marry her. She was the first woman he had ever considered marrying.

She opened the door, her face freezing with surprise. Then she peered across his shoulder making certain that the slope between them was empty. She sounded like a reprimanding teacher.

"Caleb. In broad daylight? Do you think this is wise?"

He put out a hand, an oddly imploring gesture. "I had to come. The news is too important to wait. Bart Layton went to Bedford last night. He talked to his grandfather. He tried to take the old man out."

Her frown was quick. "How can he? There's the court commitment—"

"At the point of a gun, the damned fool. We could have Thorpe swear out charges against Bart, but I don't like that idea. We don't want to call any more attention to this than we have to. But we have to do something, right away. If Ryan does get out and takes control of the mine again he'll never sell. He'd close the property first, I know him. So do you. He's as stubborn as they're born."

"Come in." She said it abruptly, remembering their exposed position on the porch. She stood aside and closed the door hurriedly after him, hoping that none of the neighbors had noticed her caller.

They faced each other across the living room, her face tight with concern. "So what's our move?"

"I'll go to Denver, set up a new syndicate with a couple of dummy managers. We will immediately sell the mine to them."

"Won't Captain Layton block such a sale?"

He hunched his shoulders. "He'll probably try. But if sixty-six and two-thirds percent of the stockholders vote to sell he can't stop it. We won't have any trouble. All Dick and Clint want is some quick money. And by luck I laid the groundwork with all three of them yesterday. I pointed out that within a month we'll run out of operating capital, that we'd have to either sell or close down. I think even Bart saw that it would be easier to sell a working property than a mine closed down and in danger of flooding."

"How much will you offer?"

He had been thinking about that, all the way up the hill. "Half a million dollars. We've got over a hundred thousand in the Denver banks, for a down payment, then we'll pay the rest out of the mine's profits."

"Captain Layton won't buy that."

"He won't have much choice. That's the way mines are bought, and everyone in the business knows it. No mining company in history ever paid more than ten percent down. We'll be offering twenty."

Mary Dorne seemed to be holding her breath.

Ever since she could remember she had hated poverty, hated the very idea of being poor. As early as she could, she had come west thinking that in a new country, where there was a shortage of women, she would be able to marry some wealthy man. But she had landed in Montrose, where there had been only one to qualify. Only Ryan Layton had had enough money to tempt her.

She would have married Ryan after his wife died, but the opportunity never came. After the accident she had hoped that by moving in here she could bring it off, on the theory that old men often fell in love with their nurses. But Ryan Layton had not even recognized her as a woman in spite of her contrived displays, wearing a loose wrapper when she tended him, letting it fall open to expose her good breasts for tantalizing seconds. The old fool had showed no more interest than if she were a wooden Indian.

She had considered the grandsons then. Clint was a gross, slobbering animal who never drew a sober breath. Even so she would have risked marriage and hoped that he would die of his excesses soon, but she had gotten nowhere there either. All Clint's needs were fulfilled by alcohol.

Dick she might have had soon after his wife had died, but Mary had had a chance to watch, to see the other woman denied even necessities while Dick lost across a card table whatever money came to him.

And then Caleb Hewmark had begun coming to see Ryan. He was big, vital, not unhandsome, and he moved her physically. No man would ever touch her deeply—she was too selfish, too grasping to surrender herself to anyone—but at least the relationship was pleasant, and she learned that he would do anything she asked, that the appeal of her body was a potent weapon there.

So the bargain had been made, and when they had the mine she would have all the money she had dreamed of owning.

Now Bart Layton had come home. And what she had thought was already in her reach might yet be lost to her. At the moment she hated him with a depth of feeling that surprised her. She could not lose now, not when she had been so close.

"Yes," she answered Hewmark. "You must act right away. If Bart Layton does find a way to bring that old man back here we'll lose everything, every chance."

"Mary." He took a quick step forward, closing his big hands over her shoulders.

She let him kiss her, judging the surge of his desire, then she pushed him away. "Not now. Someone might come. And you should be on your way at once."

"Please, Mary. I may be gone for days. . . ." He wanted her deeply in this moment, and he seldom curbed his desires, but again she was the stronger.

"You'd better see the judge before you go."
Her voice was unshaken. "You should let him
know that Captain Layton is defying his order,
that he broke into the hospital to abduct his grandfather."

He pulled his mind back to the problem, thought
about it, shook his head. "No, I can't do that. If I
said that it would only make him suspicious.
Better that we pretend to know nothing about it. I
just wish I knew what Layton will try next."

She moved out of his grasp. "I'll find out
tonight."

"Tonight?" He was suddenly jealous. "What
happens tonight?"

"I've invited Captain Layton for dinner."

"What for? What are you doing?" He reached
for her again. "If you're trying to play games with
me . . ."

She avoided his hands, stepping back
impatiently. "Don't act the fool, Caleb. We need
information. I have a way to get it. That's my
interest in the captain."

He still did not like the idea. "Anyway, I doubt
that he'll come. Ryan probably told him what he
guessed about us, or what he overheard."

"Probably."

He looked at her, hard, wondering once more
what went on behind her level eyes. He was
never sure.

"If Bart Layton knows . . . if he accuses you . . ."

She made a gesture of dismissal. "There are ways a man can be handled."

His jealousy flared again. "None of that, Mary. I won't have you making love with him."

She laughed shortly. "Sometimes you can be so stupid. There are other methods than that. A woman can make a man sorry for her, protective toward her. Don't get excited. I can manage Captain Bart Layton. Quit worrying."

Caleb Hewmark did not quit worrying. Back at his mill office he sent for Joe Gibbon. Gibbon had worked for him in Denver and followed him to Montrose. A taciturn man with a reputation both as a rough-and-tumble fighter and gun hand, Gibbon had left Denver ahead of a posse bent on hanging him. He owed his liberty, his life and his livelihood to Hewmark, but it gave him pleasure to talk back to his employer, which Hewmark accepted as being part of the price he must pay for Gibbon's work.

The hireling stood in the office, looking down on the man behind the desk, his thin-lipped mouth stretching in what for him was a grin. For another it would be a grimace.

"You still want this captain dead, huh."

Hewmark let his annoyance show. "You were supposed to do that chore at the hotel."

"Would have too, if the damned Irishman hadn't butted in."

"Never mind the excuses. I want it done."

"Then maybe you better do it yourself."

Hewmark knew Gibbon too well to let any remark he made disturb him. Gibbon had to be important, had to build up his own ego in this way, to believe himself as good as or better than Hewmark. "If you're afraid."

The truculence just below the surface broke through. "There's not a man in pants, or without pants for that matter, that I'm afraid of. Trouble with you, Caleb, you been buying your dirty work done so long you forget another man maybe wants something too."

Hewmark considered him. "What's that supposed to mean?"

"Only that I want a few cards in the game, a piece of the action."

"I don't know what you're talking about."

"When you find out, let me know." Gibbon turned on his heel and started for the door.

Hewmark let him get to the entrance before he said sharply, "Come back here."

Joe Gibbon stood for a full minute, his back to his employer, as if deciding whether he chose to obey or not. Then he turned and went slowly back to the desk.

"What's the price?"

"I been thinking," said Gibbon. "I'm thirty-four years old. I've killed six men, not counting them Indians and the two Mex that jumped me that time in El Paso. And what have I got to show for it?"

"I pay you a hundred dollars a month."

Gibbon laughed. "While you and the dame are fixing to make millions out of the Gabriel."

Hewmark's attention sharpened. He had not realized that Gibbon knew about his alliance with Mary Dorne. He did not debate it. He was a man who did not use more than enough words to make a deal.

"So?"

"So I want a third interest."

Hewmark sat very, very still. It had never occurred to him that this underling had any real ambition. He thought of the man as a work animal, a hired killer and thief, who spent his wages at the bars and found his pleasures in bedding the saloon girls.

He saw now a new side to the man, something he had not counted on. He thought of what Mary Dorne's reaction would be. It was part of the fabric of his nature to give thought to everyone who might be involved in any deal, to try to assess beforehand their reactions. Concerning the girl, he did not have to guess. He knew exactly what she would say. She would be violently opposed to anyone sharing in their bonanza. She would be as against it as he was.

He smiled then. Joe Gibbon had just signed his own death warrant.

CHAPTER TEN

Mary Dorne took a very special care with her dinner. She bought the best steak the butcher had available, took it up the hill to the house and interlarded it herself. She baked and cooked through most of the day, and set an elaborate table. She was not certain that Bart Layton would come, but she meant to be prepared, betting that the curiosity which she had read in his eyes would draw him.

And she relaxed when she saw him coming up the path, moving with a strong, pantherlike stride that ignored the steepness of the grade. She was waiting in the doorway when he reached the steps, making no pretense that she was not watching for him. She did not wait for his attack, but faced him as they came into the living room, saying bluntly, "I wasn't really sure you would come."

He raised his eyebrows, looking surprised. "I was invited, wasn't I?"

"You were. But I heard you went to the hospital last night, that you talked to Ryan."

Now his surprise was genuine. He had told no one of his visit to Bedford. "Where did you hear that?"

She lied readily. "At the butcher shop. The news is all over town."

Someone from the hospital, he thought, had

come to Montrose, and he wondered why they came and who they talked to. Aloud he said, "Why should my going there have anything to do with my coming here for dinner?"

Her laugh had an embarrassed sound. "If you talked to Ryan I can imagine what he said, that Caleb Hewmark and I are conspiring to steal the Gabriel from him. Didn't he?"

"Well . . ."

"Don't be afraid of admitting it. I feel terribly sorry for Ryan, for anyone so ill that he thinks the world has turned against him, but especially for Ryan. He is one of very few people who ever went out of their way to help me."

"You really think he's crazy then?"

She sighed deeply, sadly. "I'm not a doctor, I only know what happened to me."

"He said he overheard you and Hewmark talking over plans."

"I know. He screamed the same thing when he tried to kill me. He heard us talking, yes. He was half asleep in his chair and we were on the porch. I doubt that he could really have distinguished words . . . maybe he was full asleep . . . dreaming. He'd been muttering for days about high-grading at the mine." She saw Layton's look and met it directly. "You don't believe me."

He said honestly, "I don't know what to believe."

She nodded, coming forward to rest her fingers

lightly on his arm, so close that she had to look up at him.

"I can't blame you, coming home to such a tragedy. I'm sorry you feel uncertain of me. After the other day I'd hoped we could be friends."

Impulsively he put one hand over hers. "Why not?" He almost kissed her. He caught himself just in time. He knew that he could, but he was not ready yet. He wanted to wait, to keep his head clear for thinking.

As he left the house close to midnight she followed him onto the porch, and on the top step he turned, his head brought down level with hers.

"Thank you for the best dinner I've had in a long while. It's a surprise to find that a woman who looks like you do is so good a cook."

She laughed. "Flattery will get you another invitation. That is, if I'm here to make it."

"You're going away?"

"I may. I've been thinking about going to Denver. My place at the school had been filled, and there just aren't jobs in Montrose for a person of my limited accomplishments."

This time he did not resist his urge. He took her shoulders gently and pressed his mouth against hers, brushing the lips first, then with a rising need. He thought that she responded, but then she pushed him back, using the embarrassed laugh again.

"Captain, just because I'm a helpless female you needn't feel compelled to be gallant."

He was more shaken than he wanted to admit. "I wasn't being gallant, I—"

"Good night." Without waiting for him to finish she turned into the house and closed the door behind her, softly but solidly.

In the hall she stood with her hand on the knob, her thoughts racing. Bart Layton was a most attractive man. She reacted to him far more than she ever had to Caleb Hewmark; she could be truly interested if she let herself. Supposing the captain beat Hewmark and saved the mine? Might she not achieve her end better by marrying Layton than by working with Hewmark? She could do it, she knew, and it was a good idea for any gambler to copper her bets. Mary Dorne had long recognized that she was a gambler, a gambler who liked a sure thing.

Bart Layton stood for a long while where she had left him and then, indecisive, started down the zigzag path toward the distant street.

Some three hundred feet from the house he heard the spit of a gun, and a bullet made its whisper close by his head. In the reflex of long practice he dropped flat, drawing his own gun, landing with it in his hand. He lay quiet, tuned to listen for sound to give him a target. Then a second shot came, this from a different direction. So there were at least two of them.

Behind him the house had suddenly gone dark. He did not know what to expect, but it would certainly not be help from Mary Dorne. He could not blame her, could not ask a lone woman to respond to firing in the night. She might not even know he was under attack—yet it might be she who had set him up for this. No one else had known he was due up here tonight.

Whatever the source, he was in a bad spot, on the exposed hillside with no cover. When the moon climbed high enough to clear the eastern canyon wall they could pick him off without trouble. He continued to listen. The shots must have been heard in the town below, but there was no answering noise, no sign that anyone was coming to his aid.

Montrose, he thought, must be used to gunfire in the night now, and its citizens not about to step into what was none of their affair.

He twisted to study the rising grade, searching for a way of escape, but the ground between his exposed position and the house was as bare as though it had been scraped.

The corner of his eye caught movement off to his right. He threw a shot that way and drew three shots in return, two from the original direction, one from his left, and after the explosions the night settled into tight quiet, except for the steady rumble from the mill and the sense of the ground beneath him shaking dully to the rhythm of the stamps.

Anger rose and rode him. He did not mind a fair fight; he had enjoyed fighting through his youth, but an ambush in the dark made him coldly furious.

He had to get off the hillside. He dared not go down by the path, that was what they would expect, either that or a retreat toward the house. Years of fighting the Apaches in the bleak hills of Arizona had taught him the value of the unexpected.

Now, as if he were hunting Apaches, he began a careful inching toward the place from which the first shot had come, trying to get close enough to the bushwhacker for a clear aim. It was tedious work, wriggling on his stomach, digging his elbows into the gritty soil to drag his body forward.

What little sound he made was covered by the throbbing stamps. There was no other, nor further movement in the gloom ahead. He almost believed the attackers had given up the game and slipped away. He did not allow the thought to lull him into false security. That was what they would hope. No, they had missed, and they had not come here to fail. They too were waiting.

He had moved almost a hundred feet when he sensed the suggestion of another presence on the slope before him. It was fleeting, uncertain. He felt rather than saw that a man lay belly-down in a slight depression some twenty yards away. He froze, lying motionless, his eyes alert for the slightest movement.

It came finally. The man raised his head.

Layton fired, slamming echoes back and forth across the canyon.

A high yell drowned them, as if it were part of the gun sound, and an answering shot added to them. Bullets sprayed dirt across his face, into his eyes. The ground seemed to erupt against his head. And in that instant the gun behind him began to hammer through the night.

He felt a tug at his leg as if someone had reached out to shove it, and then a third gun took up the racket behind him, a different sound, the spit of a rifle.

His jaw tightened. Now there were three. But he concentrated on the one in front, determined to dispose of at least that one.

He saw the man half rise as if intending to run at him, and emptied his gun into the moving figure. The shape took a dozen steps, then collapsed almost within touching distance of where Layton crouched.

Bart Layton flattened again, his hurrying fingers fumbling at reloading. He lay tensed for the firing behind to continue, puzzled when it did not. Again the hillside fell silent but for its constant rumble. Then a voice called his name—a woman's voice.

"Captain! Are you all right?"

For an instant he thought it was Mary Dorne.

For an instant he thought it was a trap to draw an answer from him and expose his exact position. But the voice was not right. Then suddenly he knew who it had to be—the girl who had stopped him yesterday. Sarah Hobart.

He called softly, "I'm fine."

"I'm coming in."

"Wait." There was quick panic in his tone. "There's a man behind me."

"He's dead." She sounded as calm as if she were commenting on the weather.

He saw her movement then, and came halfway to his knees. "Watch yourself. There may be others."

"There were only the two." She still was unexcited, as if she were used to climbing across dark hillsides in the face of gunfire. Then she was beside him, crouching down as he started to rise, putting out a hand, pulling it back quickly with a small, startled gesture. "You're hit."

He had forgotten the touch at his leg. He reached down, felt the stickiness and knew that it was blood. He struck a match and in the tiny flame had a picture of her on her knees at his side, a light rifle on the ground beneath her hand.

In the flare of the match he had a look also at his leg, and quick laughter rose in his throat. The bullet had burned through the cloth a good three inches above the knee, tunneling a groove that did little more than burn the skin. For so shallow a wound it had bled excessively.

She peered at it in the brief light. "Is that all?" She sounded accusing that he had not been worse hit.

"What do you want, my head blown off?"

She was tart. "For a man who takes the chances you do, I expected a lot more damage." She rose in a single light movement.

He too came to his feet, finding no difficulty in putting his weight on the leg. "Where'd you come from?"

She was casual. "I wander around at night. What else is there to do?"

He did not answer, walking the few feet to the man he had shot. The man lay on his face. Layton used one hand to roll him over, the other to strike another match. He had never seen the face before. The girl came up while the match still burned, and Layton said, "Know him?"

"Joe Gibbon."

"Who was he?"

"Just a man. Gossip says he's a gunfighter, that he got run out of Denver."

Layton dropped the match. "What was he doing in Montrose?"

Her voice was dry. "Trying to kill you, it seems."

He could not see her small face distinctly. It was only a white blur. "You knew what he was doing?"

"I saw them start up the hill. They're a pair, Gibbon and the one they call Rudy. The one I shot, over there."

Layton knew a surge of unreality. Two men he had never heard of ambushing him, and a girl who did not look strong enough to carry a rifle, let alone to fire it, quietly saying she had killed one of them. He crossed and found the second body and used another match. Rudy had a hole through his head. Layton said flatly, "Either you're lucky or you've got sharper eyes than I have."

"Paw claims I've got cat eyes. I can see in the dark better than most." The voice was still grave.

He straightened from examining the dead man. "Did you know I was up here?"

"I knew."

"How?"

"I saw you going to her place. You're like all the rest."

"What rest?"

"The men. All she has to do is flick those petticoats and they go swarming around her. I thought maybe you'd be different."

"Just why did you think that?"

For once she seemed to have difficulty finding the words she wanted. "I don't know. I just hoped so."

"Why?"

She still fumbled. "I guess I just thought you were the last chance. If you didn't have any sense there wasn't any chance for Montrose."

"Who are all these men who are interested in Miss Dorne?"

"Everybody."

"You mean every man in town? She must be very popular with the wives. It's a wonder they'd let her stay here."

The girl moved restlessly, hedging her accusation. "Well, most of the single ones, I mean. They used to hang around the school when she was teaching." She barked a short laugh. "They wasted their time. She never gave any of them the time of day."

"Is Caleb Hewmark one of them?"

She was uncertain there. "I can't say about that. He used to come up here a lot when your grandather was home. Lately I haven't seen him much."

"And you watch the house all the time?"

Now she turned defensive. "We live right down at the bottom of the hill. I kind of see when people pass our place. Hewmark came up this morning."

Layton's attention sharpened. "He did? Was he in a hurry? Did he seem excited? How long did he stay?"

"Not very long."

"Sarah," he said, "I want to get off this hill, and I think you and I have a little talk coming. Where can we go?"

"To our place. I'll give you a cup of coffee."

"I got the idea your father didn't want me there."

"He's at the mine, working."

"I thought they weren't working the night shift?"

"They're not, not the full crew, but they have to keep a skeleton to run the pumps and the lifts and such. He takes turns. One week he's on nights, the next he works days."

"All right, your place. And I can use that coffee."

He followed her down the dark trail, guided by her sure-footed shadow across the ground that he could hardly see. He waited in the doorway while she lighted the lamp, went in as she took the blackened coffee pot from the back of the stove and poured the black liquid into two thick mugs.

"No cream. There's not a cow in fifty miles."

He gave her a crooked grin. "Never was, that I can remember."

"I keep forgetting you were raised here. You act different from these people."

"Oh? How's that?"

Her thin shoulders moved under the cotton shirt, but she was incapable of evasion. "Probably because you went away, saw more than they see. And because you were an army officer."

"It doesn't change a man to put him in uniform." He sat down at the scrubbed table. The place was uncommonly clean, the cleanest room he had seen since coming back to the town. He said abruptly, "You know, you're a strange person yourself."

"What's strange about me?"

"Well, for one thing, your concern with the town."

"It isn't the town, it's the people, with everything they own invested here. They're what I'm fighting for."

She looked so small, so intense, so feisty that he broke into laughter. "A town tamer. A regular town tamer."

She was angered. "It isn't funny when people are going to lose all they've got."

"I didn't think it was funny." His voice was mild. "I stand to lose too . . . my interest in the Gabriel."

"It's not the same with you."

"No?" He looked at her quizzically. "Twice I've been ambushed, and someone killed the only real friend I ever had. Isn't that enough to lose?"

She was at once contrite. "I meant that the miners who haven't anything except their houses and their pay are more helpless than you. You have so much; you're Ryan Layton's grandson—"

"And broke. I got fired from the army. Did you know that, Sarah?"

Once more she bridled. "You're having fun with me again. Nobody ever got fired from the army, Captain."

"Nobody but Bart Layton. Can I ask your help?"

Her eyes grew larger, darker. "How?"

"I talked to Ryan last night. I don't think he's crazy. Do you?"

"I never did. Because *she* said he was and I don't believe a word she says."

His tone was dry. "I'm beginning to get the idea you don't really like her."

"I don't like anyone who's two-faced. Oh, I know, you don't believe that, you're just like all men. Give you a pretty face and legs and breasts and you all lose your minds."

He didn't know whether to kiss her or spank her, and covered the moment by finishing his coffee, changing the subject.

"I haven't thanked you for saving my life."

"Don't bother. I'm sorry I did."

"Your privilege. But I'm still asking your help. I don't know much about mining, and people, including you, keep saying the Gabriel's being high-graded. But at the same time they say the ore is so complex that you can't extract the gold unless you cyanide it."

She bobbed her head. "Paw calls it ornery ore. That's his word for ore that's hard to dress."

"Does he think there's stealing going on?"

She was silent.

"Why doesn't he want you to talk to me about it?"

She said sharply, "You've got no right to ask me to talk against my own father."

"Against?" He took a shot in the dark. "Is he in on it? Is that what worries you?"

"It is not. My father never stole anything in his life."

"Then why doesn't he want you to talk?"

He thought she was not going to answer, it took so long for the words to come; then they came in a choked gasp.

"He's afraid."

"Of what?"

"Being fired. If Hewmark gets control of the mine. He has a lot of friends, he can get a man blacklisted so he could never work underground again."

"And he believes Hewmark will get control?"

She nodded.

"Do you think so?"

Again the nod.

"Then I don't understand you. You don't want the town to die, and if Hewmark does get control the mine won't close, will it?"

"It might as well."

"What does that mean?"

"Paw worked in a mine Hewmark ran in Clifton. He paid the lowest wages in the territory. Most of the men struck and they broke the strike."

"Your father didn't go out with them?"

She shook her head viciously. "My father's nerve is gone, I tell you. Now, get the hell out of here. I've talked too much."

CHAPTER ELEVEN

There was no light in Sheriff Fred Foster's house, a low, single-story structure of logs and rough-sawed timber with a split-shake roof.

Bart Layton used the butt of his gun to pound on the plank door. Light came up within and a thin woman in a worn wrapper pulled the door open a few inches, peering out.

"Is Fred here?"

"He's sleeping." The voice was thin, harried, bitter. "He was out all afternoon hunting the hills for the man who held up the Traytown stage."

Layton had not heard of the holdup. "I'm sorry, but this is important. There are two dead men up on the Layton hill."

She peered for another long moment of brooding silence, debating, he guessed, the chance that if she closed the door he would go away and let her husband rest. Then, in resignation, she said, "I'll tell him."

She left the door ajar, but did not ask him in. Fred Foster pulled the panel wide in a few minutes, fastening his pants, scrubbing at his sleep-puffed eyes and tousled hair.

"Two dead men on the hill, you say? Who killed them?"

Layton hesitated for the barest instant, deciding

to keep the girl out of it. He owed her that. "I did."

Foster blinked, frowning. "This is getting kind of regular, Bart. First the man at the hotel, now two more."

"They were shooting at me." Layton said it without emotion.

"Why? Who were they? When did it happen?"

He could not admit knowing their names without saying how he knew them. He lied again, thinking how one lie breeds another. "Bushwhackers still trying to kill me. Little over an hour ago."

Foster, studying him, turned suddenly hostile. "And what were you doing on the hill at this time of night?"

"I'd been up at my grandfather's place."

"To see Mary Dorne?"

"She's living there."

"Did she see the shooting?"

"I doubt it. I was quite a way below the house when they cut loose. Her lights were out."

Foster shook his head as if to clear it of the dregs of sleep. "I don't get this. Oh, I'm not saying it isn't the truth, but why the devil does anyone want you dead?"

Layton said flatly. "The mine."

"Now wait a minute—"

"You wait," said Layton, his patience run out. "I went over to Bedford to see Ryan last night—"

"They won't let anyone see him."

107

"I saw him. I went over the stockade."

"That's illegal and you know it. The hospital is private property."

Bart Layton lost his temper. "Fred, what in hell has happened to you? I never thought I'd live to see the day when you turned chicken. Go ahead, arrest me for breaking in to see the old man, instead of wondering who is hiring men to shoot me."

From behind the sheriff the wife whined, "You don't understand, Captain."

Layton swung on her. "And what is it that I don't understand now?"

"Fred is a law officer. Oh, I've heard the tales about how wild you and he were when you were young, but some people have to grow up. Fred has responsibilities, if you don't."

With difficulty Layton checked his sharp retort, and said steadily, "Ryan Layton is as sane as either of us, Fred. I'll take my oath on that. They've got him cooped up worse than in prison. They don't tie you to a bed in jail."

He saw the sheriff's eyes change and recognized that Foster was having difficulty living with himself. He knew suddenly that it was the wife, not the man who made the decisions in this house. As if to confirm the guess, Foster turned to glance at the woman before he answered.

"I hope you're right, Bart. I hope you can get him out."

"I mean to." Layton was grim. "I'd have done it today, but the judge went to Denver last night. I wouldn't leave my worst enemy in that hell-hole. If I were you I'd investigate it, find out just how well Doctor Thorpe treats his patients. And while you're doing it you might find out just who is paying what to keep my grandfather out of reach of anyone."

This outraged the sheriff himself. "Now look here. Ryan was sent there on a legitimate court order. I answered the call myself when he tried to cut the Dorne girl, and you should have heard him rave. Maybe he isn't crazy now, but he certainly was then."

"What do you think of Mary Dorne?"

The question caught Foster off guard. "What do I think of her?"

"I understand from good authority that half the men in Montrose are in love with her."

The sheriff's face reddened and he glanced quickly at his wife, quickly away.

She said tartly, "Who told you that?"

Layton shook his head. "It was said in confidence." He thought, If you want to know about one woman, ask another.

Mrs. Foster's waspish tone went on. "Maybe she told you herself. It would be like her."

"No, it was someone else."

"Then it must have been one of your cousins, them letting her live on up there where she's no right. And I'd hate to think that many men were making fools of themselves. Most, I'd say, have better sense."

"Which sort would you say was Caleb Hewmark?"

"Mr. Hewmark is a brilliant man and he has done a great deal for Montrose and I have never, ever heard his name mentioned in the same breath with that of that school teacher."

The sharp voice so warmed when it spoke of Hewmark that it warned Layton. Any trouble between himself and Hewmark would find the sheriff on the other side. He wondered how many others in town would feel the same; a number, he expected.

He walked with Fred Foster up the hill in uncomfortable silence. Foster had called in two deputies, one of them bringing a small buckboard. Between them they loaded the bodies into the box, then one deputy drove to the undertaker and the other returned with Layton and Foster to the street. At the bottom of the hill Layton said, "I'll buy a drink."

The deputy looked hopeful, but Foster shook his head. "I'm beat. I spent eight hours in the saddle, and that's more riding than I've done in a year. Besides, Myrtle doesn't like me to drink at night, says the smell of liquor on my breath makes her dizzy."

Layton watched him go, taking the deputy with

him, probably to save him from Bart's temptations. Then, alone, he turned in at the saloon.

There was no one at the bar. Terry Roark was standing, watching the play at the only poker table running. He heard the batwing doors flap open, looked across his shoulder and then moved up behind the long counter, set out the bottle and two glasses without being asked.

Layton poured two drinks, taking his attention from the poker table. Of the six men there his cousin Dick made one, seated with his back to the rear wall. At the moment he was dealing, and from his expression and the small stack of chips on the cloth before him, Bart guessed that he was losing.

Roark picked up his glass but did not raise it to his lips, waiting for Bart. Layton raised his and they drank together, with a touch of ceremony. Bart poured a second, saying in a low voice, not looking at the bartender, "What do you know about a man named Joe Gibbon?"

Roark's lips did not appear to move behind the shelter of the drooping mustache. "What about him?"

"He's dead."

"Ah," said Terry Roark. "It couldn't have happened to one who was more deserving. How did he die?"

"I shot him. He tried to dry-gulch me."

The bartender savored the second drink, gazed

at the small glass reflectively as if he could learn something from it.

"Our town is rapidly becoming a better place since you arrived."

"Tell me about Gibbon."

"Nothing unusual to tell. Every town has its Joe Gibbons. They gamble a little, drink a lot, and kill to feel they're as good as decent men."

"Who did he work for?"

Roark put down the glass, picked up his rag and mopped at the already spotless bar. "Work. Depends on what you mean by the term. In the two years since he showed up here I'll gamble he has done not a single hour of what is generally considered work."

"All right, who did he kill for?"

"Now that's another question entirely. A strange thing. Whenever a man made trouble at the mine and something happened to him, it was usually Joe Gibbon who picked the fight."

"He was working for my cousins, you mean?"

"Do you believe they have a word of say in the running of the mine?"

"I don't. So you're talking about Hewmark?"

"Maybe. But I've got no proof and I was never a one to point the finger when I wasn't sure."

"Thanks," said Layton. "I wouldn't want you to. I wouldn't ask that of any man."

"But if I had to speak of someone," the Irishman went on, "I wouldn't know who else it could be."

Layton laid a coin on the bar, but Roark pushed it back.

"On the house."

Again Layton said, "Thanks." He turned toward the door, then stopped. A chair at the poker table had been pushed back.

He heard Dick Layton say, "That finished me," saw him stand, walk around the table, and apparently discover Bart for the first time.

"Hey." Dick came up. "Where'd you come from? I've been looking for you all evening."

"I've been standing right here for fifteen minutes."

Dick shrugged. "When I'm playing I don't see anything around me. Not that it does me any good. I've done nothing but lose for the last month." The tone was sour.

"You could quit."

"What? When I'm behind? That's crazy. Luck runs in cycles. Come on, I want to talk to you." In a swift change of mood to one of pent-up excitement, he led the way out to the deserted street and turned toward the hotel.

Bart said, "About what?"

"Something wonderful has happened. We'll go up to Clint's room. The bum is probably drunk, but we can wake him up, get it all settled right now. Hewmark wants an answer in the morning."

"Answer to what?"

"Are you ready for some good news? He's found a buyer for the Gabriel, went to Denver this morning, yesterday, to see them. He wired me this evening. That's why I've been hunting you."

"What are they offering?"

There was a hushed quality in Dick's voice now, as if he could not believe the good fortune.

"Five hundred thousand dollars. Five."

Bart Layton stopped in the middle of the sidewalk. He could not see his cousin's face in the heavy gloom.

"I don't believe it."

"I'll show you the wire as soon as we get up to Clint's."

"Oh, I believe you got the wire. But I don't believe Hewmark would sell the mine for five hundred thousand. He loaned it two hundred and fifty thousand and took a quarter interest in place of payment. If it's sold for five he'd get only a fourth, one hundred and twenty-five, for himself, and lose the other hundred-twenty-five thousand. I can't see him doing a thing like that. There has to be something else about all this, something we don't know about."

CHAPTER TWELVE

Clint Layton was as drunk as expected. He lay on top of the bed, clothed except for his shirt, his huge stomach swelling like a balloon beneath the underwear. Dick lit the lamp and looked down on his brother without love.

"Look at what the damn fool's doing to himself."

Bart thought it was too bad Dick could not stand aside and see what gambling had done to him, but talking to a compulsive gambler was as useless as talking to a compulsive drinker.

Dick was shaking the big man ungently, saying, "Wake up, you souse. Come out of it. We're selling the Gabriel."

Clint's eyes opened and stared at his brother between puffy lids, disoriented for a long minute. Then with a groan he rolled to sit up.

"Can't it wait until morning?"

"The telegram said the syndicate wants an answer by noon."

"What syndicate?"

"I tried to tell you earlier, but you were too liquored up to know what I was saying. Have you slept enough now to follow an idea?"

Clint looked about him, spotted the half-full bottle on the floor beside the bed and bent to reach it. Dick got it first, set it on the dresser.

"Not until we get this thing arranged."

Clint sulked. "Well, what's the deal?"

"Five hundred thousand for the mine. One hundred and twenty-five thousand for each of us."

Clint's dull eyes lighted.

"Enough," Dick went on, "to get us out of this miserable town. We can go to Denver, San Francisco, anywhere we want to."

Bart Layton had lingered beside the doorway. He said quietly, "I am not selling until I know a lot more about what's going on than I do now."

Clint's big head swung heavily, the loose lips agape. He had not known that Bart was there. He sounded peevish as a child. "Where'd you come from?"

Dick cut in in disgust. "He came up with me, and he's selling, whether he likes it or not."

Bart's smile was a thin twisting of the lips. "Just how do you intend to make me?"

"I don't have to. For your information, two-thirds of the shareholders of a company can take action without the agreement of the other third. With Hewmark's vote we control seventy-five percent. How do you think you can stop us?"

Bart did not know the law, made no pretense of it. He said, "Hewmark dreamed up the deal, so of course he'll vote with you. But how do you know he's not buying the Gabriel himself?"

The cousins looked at him blankly. Dick

laughed. "That's absurd. What would he use for money?"

"Is this wire offering cash?"

Dick pulled the yellow sheet from his pocket and read, accenting each word. "Syndicate of bankers and mining men offer five hundred thousand for Gabriel. One hundred thousand down, balance in installments to be arranged . . ."

"Meaning that they expect to pay the installments out of the mine's profits. And if there are no profits, they turn it back, right?"

Again they stared.

"What's the rest of it?"

Dick went on, slowly now. "Advise we act at once. Offer good only through tomorrow. We will only be able to meet one more payroll."

"So you don't get a hundred and twenty-five apiece . . . you get twenty-five."

They looked at each other uncertainly. Then Dick shrugged.

"But we get it. And if they turn the mine back we can keep the twenty-five. That's better than having the mine close."

Bart apparently did not hear. "So Hewmark would buy the mine for seventy-five thousand, split three ways between us."

"If he's buying it himself."

"You're a gambling man, Dick. If I was going for the deal I'd bet my share against yours that he is, but I'm not going for it. Here's what I'll do instead. I'll buy both your shares, give you twenty-five thousand each down and the rest from profits, same as this offer."

Dick Layton hooted. "Where you going to get that kind of money?"

"I'll get it. Will you sell to me? I don't want this Denver crowd in here, as absentee owners. The mine belongs to the town."

Dick was shaking his head. "I don't get you, Bart. What do you care whether it's owned by people in Denver or New York or China? Montrose doesn't mean anything to you. You've been gone for years."

Bart Layton started to answer, then checked himself. What did he care? What did the town mean to him? There was no pleasure in his childhood memories. Why should he worry, as long as he came out with his share of the mine? Then he heard Sarah Hobart's voice talking fiercely about the miners who relied on the Gabriel, who would be cut to starvation wages if Hewmark's crowd took over.

"I've just learned that a man has to care about something, Dick," he said. "He has to believe in something on which he can build a life. Ryan believed in the Gabriel. He built this town. And no matter what he did to me, he paid fair wages, made his town prosper."

Dick's laugh was raw. "You sound like a preacher."

118

"Never mind how I sound. Will you sell to me?"

Dick looked at his brother, got only a vacant gape for answer, and finally grinned.

"Why not? It will do me good to watch you fall flat on your face. I never liked you, cousin mine. You got away with stuff as a kid that I couldn't manage, you ran out and left us for Ryan to pick on. In fact, my friend, I hate your guts. But you'd better have the money by noon or it's no deal."

Bart Layton turned without a word, went into the hall and stopped there for a long minute, thinking, before he went toward his room. He had less than a hundred dollars in his pocket. Still, that was a lot more than Ryan had when he started the Gabriel.

At nine o'clock the next morning he walked into the office of the bank. It did not open for general business until nine-thirty, but Blakestone Heath was already at his desk, rising to extend his hand.

"Well, Bart. What can I do for you this morning?"

Bart did not sit down. "You can loan me seventy-five thousand dollars."

Heath made a practice of never showing surprise, but this was past his control. "Loan you . . . what are you planning, buying all of Colorado?"

"Only the Gabriel."

Layton sat down then and shoved across the desk the copy of the telegram he had picked up at the telegraph office. The banker read it twice before he looked up.

"So?"

"Whoever these men are, they apparently believe the mine is worth half a million dollars."

"At least they're putting up a hundred thousand."

"True. So if it's worth that to them it's worth it to me."

"With one difference. I judge from the request that you do not possess a hundred thousand dollars'?"

"You judge right. Did you ever look at the vouchers they pay army officers with?"

The banker's smile was thin. "I've heard rumors. And frankly, I don't know about this loan."

"What's the matter with it? If the Denver men—"

Heath held up one hand. "Have you ever before had occasion to apply for a bank loan?"

Layton shook his head.

"Then perhaps you don't know. I don't have the authority to make such a loan on my own. It's up to the loan committee."

"Who are they? How long will it take?"

"There are seven on the committee, all merchants, all stockholders in the bank. They meet once a week, they met yesterday and won't get together again until next week."

Layton's heart sank. "I've got to know by noon. My cousins won't wait beyond that."

"And I doubt that the committee would look favorably on a loan to buy the mine. There have been rumors about it floating for months."

Layton could find no answer.

"And there's another thing. In making a loan we're governed as much by the borrower and his reputation and experience as we are by the collateral. Bart, while I respect you, you don't know much about operating a mine. The Gabriel seems at best to be a marginal operation. If this Denver crowd buys it they'll have the best management and probably adequate capital to modernize. Supposing I did loan you the purchase price, what would you do for payroll money and such?"

Layton drew a long, deep breath. "I don't know. . . . I . . ."

"So maybe it's best for all concerned if you take this offer. At least you and your cousins will get something."

Layton knew a desperation, a feeling he had never before experienced. It had seemed so simple when he talked to Dick the night before. The bank would loan him the money; he would throw out Hewmark's men and take over. He would discover how the high-grading had been done.

"These merchants," he said, "these men on the loan committee, they have businesses in Montrose. Certainly they won't want to see the town die."

Heath spread his hands. "Of course not, Bart, but they won't look at it as if it's dying. They'll be happy to have this new syndicate in, with fresh money, to increase production."

"Even though the new crowd cuts the miners' wages?"

The banker shrugged. "Few people see that far ahead."

Layton was like a fighter driven into a corner, hemmed in by the ropes.

"What if we don't sell? What if we merely close the mine?"

The banker frowned. "How could you manage that?"

"I can't. Ryan Layton can, if I get him out of that hospital. He still owns the mine."

A genuine interest sparked in Heath's eyes. "You think he's sane enough now?"

"I'm certain of it. I'm going to the judge as soon as he gets back."

Heath studied the ceiling, pursing his lips. "That might change the picture. It just might. For one thing, you wouldn't have to buy out your cousins. If Ryan is ruled sane, he owns all the stock except what Hewmark holds."

"And you would trust him to run the mine right?"

"Even from a wheelchair, yes. You bring him back and if he asks for it I think we can arrange for operating capital."

Layton left the bank and walked to the courthouse, met Fred Foster in the lower hall and learned that the judge was not expected until evening. Then Foster tapped his chest.

"Those men you shot . . . the District Attorney wants a statement."

"I told you what happened."

"Sure, I know, but Frank Rudy's on the warpath. He says he'll kill you on sight."

"Who's he?"

"Brother of one of the dead men. The other was Joe Gibbon, who wasn't much loss. Neither was Rudy, for that matter, but his brother is. He's head of the miners' union and a very tough customer."

"Maybe he knows who they were working for."

"Frank says they weren't working for anyone."

"Just taking an evening stroll on the mountain?"

Foster looked at him, then away. "Better go tell the D.A. your story before he swears out a warrant I'll have to serve on you."

The District Attorney was named Wymer, and he had come to town after Layton had left. A thin man with an austere face and steel-rimmed glasses, he peered at Bart with the intentness of a nervous chipmunk.

"You've been a little busy since you came back, Captain."

Layton did not like him. The man reminded him unfavorably of several army officers he had known.

"A little. Apparently people don't like me."

"Three men dead, and a complaint from Doctor Thorpe that you broke into his hospital and manhandled his staff."

Layton looked at him without speaking.

"We've had a quiet town for years here, and we like it that way."

Still Layton was silent.

"Do you want to tell me what happened?"

"I've already told Fred Foster. I was at Mary Dorne's for dinner. When I left, the two men shot at me."

"And you killed them."

"I guess so. It was dark, but they are dead."

"One by a rifle bullet, one with a forty-five. Do you usually carry a rifle when you go to dinner?"

Layton shrugged.

"You know," said Wymer, "I have the strangest feeling you're not telling the whole truth. Foster talked with Miss Dorne. She admitted that you'd been there for dinner, but she says you left a good hour before the killing. She isn't even certain she heard the shots. She'd been asleep and can't be sure."

Layton had been controlling his rising temper with difficulty. He said shortly, "If that's the way she wants it. You can't call a pretty woman a liar."

"You mean she is?"

"Her memory doesn't match with mine."

"That doesn't answer my question. I think that

for some reason of your own you killed Gibbon and Rudy, and I think you had help."

"Think what you want to." The talk was pointless, and Layton stood up. "Am I under arrest?"

"It might be the best thing, for your own protection. Frank Rudy has a lot of friends."

"I'll watch them."

"As soon as the judge gets back I'm going to ask him to put both you and Rudy under a peace bond, until we find out what's going on. I'm not going to have open warfare on the streets of Montrose."

Layton stood looking down on the man for a long moment, then he swung out of the office and down the creaking stairs. He crossed the road and moved with a hard stride down to the mill, trying to walk out his anger. He had not been near the mine yet, and to the mill only on his visit to Hewmark.

He came into the big, rambling building and paused at the office, where a small, bald-headed man sat behind a high desk, making out ore delivery reports. The round, cherubic face was expressionless, looking up as Bart stopped.

"Help you?"

"Who's in charge?"

"Why, I guess I am. I'm the superintendent."

"What's your name?"

The round face took on a hint of red. "And just who are you, to be asking questions?"

"The name is Layton. Bart Layton."

The man's manner altered. "Oh, you're the one who just came home? Sorry, I didn't realize. . . . What can I do?"

"I'd like to see the mill."

The man put down his pen and led Bart into the cyanide room, where the pulverized ore from the ball mill was dumped into settling tanks.

The mill was built on three levels, following the rising contour of the canyonside. At the top the carts from the mine brought down the broken ore and fed it into the chutes which let it down by gravity to the stone floor where the iron-shod stamps broke it to a size to be handled by the jaw crushers. Then from the crushers it slid down again over the sorting screens to the ball mills to be ground into powder. It was, Layton saw, as efficient a process as could be devised. The mill employed only some ten men on each shift. The rest was done automatically.

Below the cyanide room were the furnaces where the sludge skimmed from the tanks was fired, the recovered molten gold poured into bars, readied for shipment to the Denver mint.

The door guarding the room where these bars were collected was of heavy planks, bolted to massive hinges and fastened by twin locks.

Layton, studying it, asked, "Why two locks?"

"It was Mr. Hewmark's idea. He has one key, Dick Layton has the other. The door can't be opened unless both of them are here."

126

Layton nodded slowly. "Sounds like a good idea. Thanks for showing me around."

He left the mill and walked up the main street to the hotel, passing a dozen people, conscious that each of them turned to look after him. He wondered how many were Frank Rudy's friends, how many were pondering the best way to kill him.

In the town where he had been raised, he felt, he had not now a single friend. Terry Roark. . . . He had no illusion that the bartender would choose sides in case of real trouble. No, there was not a friend . . . Sarah Hobart. . . .

Thought of the girl brought a quick smile. Then he sobered. It was she, not himself, who had killed Frank Rudy's brother. He would have to see her, warn her that neither Foster nor the District Attorney knew of her part in the night's violence.

It was noon when Layton climbed the hotel stairs and went into Clint's room. Clint sat heavily in the sagging bed, Dick in a chair beside the window. He was surprised to see a glass in Dick's hand, a partly filled bottle on the floor at his side. He had never seen this cousin take more than one drink. Dick had maintained that a gambler, as he considered himself, could not afford to cloud his brain with alcohol. But one glance told him that the man was now well on the way to being drunk.

Clint was without a shirt, his stomach stretching

the buttons and buttonholes of his underwear. He held a bottle in his fat hand, not troubling with a glass. He raised it to drink, then winked.

"Celebrating. Did you get the money?"

"I did not."

Their faces went blank. Both heads swiveled to the wall clock. Dick said, "Your time's up. I'm going down and send that wire to Hewmark to close the deal."

"No."

Dick stood up, his voice grave with the liquor he had consumed. "What do you mean, no? We gave you your chance, you said you could raise the money. You fell on your face, like I expected."

"That's right."

"So we sell, and there's not one damned thing you can do to prevent it."

Layton held his control. "There is. And I will do it as soon as the judge gets here."

Clint got up now, wobbly, blinking owlishly. "And what does that mean?"

"I'm going to bring grandfather home and have the trust the court established set aside. When he's declared sane he'll still own the mine, and I'll bet you anything you want to name that nothing in this world will make him sell his mine."

Dick drew a long, steadying breath. "You're the one who's lost his mind now. Ryan was as crazy as they come when they took him away; he'd been getting worse ever since the accident. You couldn't talk to him, he wouldn't listen, all he'd talk about was his obsession that someone was stealing from the property."

"Maybe they were."

"How? How?"

"I don't know. Yet. But then, I don't know as much about the Gabriel as he does."

Clint blustered. "The old fool starved us to death, never would let us spend a nickel for anything."

"Meaning booze."

"Wait a minute." It was Dick, sounding strained. "Let's use our heads. Maybe you're right, maybe we are being taken on this sale, but at least we get something. And if you bring Ryan back, what do you do for operating capital?"

"With Ryan running things I can get it from the bank."

"Did Heath tell you so?"

"He did."

"He talked out of turn. He doesn't have the say. The merchants control the bank. And, Bart, Hewmark has power with the merchants."

"Nevertheless, I am bringing Ryan home."

Dick's temper was slipping. "And what happens to Clint and me then? He'll throw us out in the street." His eyes narrowed, turned crafty. "Maybe that's what you want. Maybe you figure on bringing him back even if he isn't all there and using him as a front, to get rid of us and have the whole thing for yourself."

Bart Layton's tone was thick with contempt. "Is it beyond you that a man should do something because he believes it's right, not merely to gain himself?"

"It doesn't happen in this world, and you're a fool if you think it does."

"And supposing I go along with you, agree to sell. Suppose the deal is worked out, what happens to Ryan then?"

"What do you mean, what happens to him?"

"Does he stay in that hospital, tied to that bed?"

"What's the difference?" Dick waved his hand. "They feed him, keep him clean. He's an old man, crippled, no good to anyone including himself. Now, damn it, I'm going to send that wire."

"I said you weren't."

"You try to stop me."

He thrust toward the door and Bart grabbed his shoulder as he passed. Dick pivoted with surprising speed. One hand had been kept in his pocket. It appeared, holding a small thirty-eight. He backed away, his face a mask of fury.

"I'm going to kill you. There's been nothing but trouble ever since you showed up. I'm going to kill you, and everybody in this town will thank me."

"Put it down."

Bart took a slow step toward his cousin. He was confident that he could pull his own gun from the holster at his hip and fire before Dick could pull his trigger more than once. The chances were that a single bullet from the light gun wouldn't stop him unless it found the heart or head, and he had a poor opinion of Dick as a gunman. Still, it was a chance, and further, he did not want to kill his relative.

"Put it down." He repeated it, taking another step, trying to get Dick to talk. The longer a man waited after he drew a gun the less likelihood there was that he would actually fire.

He hadn't counted on Clint. Behind him the fat man moved. He still held his bottle and stepped forward, his sock feet making no warning sound on the rough floor boards. The bottle swung and shattered as it was brought down along the side of Bart's head.

The blow stunned Layton. He dropped to his knees, caught his weight on his hands, barely kept from falling forward onto his face. He stayed there, moving his head slowly in a futile effort to clear it.

Dick stood a moment, shocked by surprise, then with a grunting laugh he came in quickly, drove a kick at Bart's head.

Bart saw the movement. He put up a hand to ward off the swinging foot, caught it instead, and pushed. Thrown off balance, Dick went down at his side, the gun flipped into the air and clattered under the bed.

The man landed on his back, air driven out of

him, but they came up together, Dick throwing a fist. It caught Bart on the ear, jarred him sidewise, but he kept his feet. He hammered one blow into Dick's stomach, another toward his jaw, which missed and landed in the neck.

They closed then, both swinging wildly without thought of self-protection, beating at each other's heads and bodies. Dick was blinded by rage, the lift the unaccustomed whiskey had given him fading under the pounding of Bart's fists.

Bart Layton too was temporarily blinded, by blood running down from the gash the bottle had cut in his scalp. But after his first quick surge of anger he had himself under the control of reason. He dashed the blood from his eyes, his head cleared and he went to work with care, making each blow tell, avoiding his cousin's wilder swings, taking some of them on the shoulder, some on his forearm.

Twice Dick's hard fist cracked solidly on his jaw, sending him backward against the far wall. The second time he jumped in on the rebound, hooking a right to the head, a left to the stomach, driving the air out of the other's lungs.

Dick staggered. He grabbed the post of the iron bed for support, standing there trying to steady his balance. In that instant Clint jumped on Bart's back.

The very weight of the fat man bulldogged them both to the floor. Clint had wrapped his massive arms around Bart's shoulders, trying to pinion him.

Bart wrenched free of the grip, rolled away from the fat man and struggled up as Dick charged him again. Grimly he set himself to knock his cousin out. He had no illusion about the alternatives. They would kill him if they could. He stood in their way; they were frightened that somehow he would cost them their interests in the Gabriel.

His swinging fist crushed into Dick's nose, flattening it. Blood splattered over him. His next blow closed an eye. He was amazed at the punishment Dick could absorb and stay on his feet. The man's arms were still flailing, but now to no purpose, striking out with no power behind the blows. Bart stepped inside and hit him squarely on the jaw, a right and then a left.

Dick Layton went down. He seemed to crumble rather than fall, his knees bent, his arms flapped, but he made no effort to catch himself as he sank.

He landed on his side, then rolled slowly onto his face. Bart wiped the blood and sweat from his eyes with the back of his hand. He turned in time to see Clint lumbering to his feet, to see that he had rescued the gun from under the bed.

Before he could lift it, Bart Layton was on him with the fury of a hunting cat. The sight of the gun turned his full anger on the fat man. Deliberately he beat him until Clint collapsed, a whimpering hulk.

He stood then, his legs wide, tasting the blood from his cut head, his bruised lips, feeling the anger drain out of him slowly. He had beaten both of them into unconsciousness. But the fight was not finished. It had barely begun.

CHAPTER THIRTEEN

Noon came and passed. Caleb Hewmark lingered at the telegraph office waiting for his answer. He could not imagine Dick and Clint Layton refusing the bait he had dangled before them. When he could stand the strain no longer he wired the telegraph operator in Montrose, a man he kept in his pay.

"Find Dick Layton. Have him contact me."

An hour later he was answered. "Dick and Clint both unable to leave doctor's office after fight with Captain Layton."

Caleb Hewmark read, and reread in mounting anger, cursing aloud. He would have to return to Montrose immediately, to find out what was going on. The stage would be too slow. He hired a horse.

The town toward which he galloped was boiling as news of the Layton fight flew from mouth to mouth. The sheriff heard it and started out to look for Bart. The District Attorney heard it and went to Foster's office to swear out a warrant. Frank Rudy heard it and send out a call to his friends for help. And Sarah Hobart heard it from a miner who came to the house to summon her father.

At once she too went in search of Layton. He was not at the hotel. He was not in the doctor's office. He was not at the saloon.

While these several citizens searched for him, each for his own reason, Bart Layton sat on a pile of hay in a rear stall of old Andy's livery stable.

He had not gone there to hide. After the fight he had left the hotel by the rear door to avoid being seen in his bloodied condition. And as he went up the alley Andy had hailed him from the back of the barn.

"What happened to you? Frank Rudy's buddies catch you?"

Bart Layton stopped, giving the hostler a twisting smile. "Not Rudy. I had a slight argument with a couple of relations."

"Come on in here and let me get you washed up." The old man brought a bucket of water and swabbed the dirt and crusted blood from Layton's head. "Somebody sure marked you."

"Dick did."

Andy whistled. "I didn't think he had it in him. Boy, you sure have raised hell around this place. If you're smart you'll let me saddle your horse and ride out while you can. Frank Rudy's a mean customer. I remember when he first come here, he'd been in trouble in California and he started more here. He kept it going until your grandfather made a deal with him. It's too bad you had to kill his no-good brother."

Layton said nothing, finishing washing his hands, touching the tender spots on his cheeks.

Andy watched him speculatively. "How you feel?"

"Like I'd been in a fight."

"What you going to do now?"

"See the judge, as soon as he gets in town."

"Then you'd better hole up here. He always brings his team in first thing after a trip."

Layton stayed. He lay back on the hay and felt the dull ache of every bone in his body. He could not recall any fight in which he had taken so much punishment.

Twice men came to the barn to ask the hostler if he had been there. Then, about five, he heard another voice talking in the runway.

"I've got to find him." The girl's voice was tense. Layton did not recognize it at first, listening to the subdued murmur between her and Andy without really hearing the words, half asleep. "He's got to be warned. There's a mob growing in the saloon and Rudy is feeding them all the liquor they can hold. If they find him now he's a dead man."

Layton came fully awake. It was Sarah Hobart, talking about him. He almost stood up to look over the wall of the stall.

Andy was saying, "Keep out of this, kid. It's not your affair."

The fierceness of her tone increased. "Don't be an old fool, Andy. Layton did not kill Frank's brother. I did."

Layton heard Andy's gasp. He stood up then and the girl saw him. For a full moment there was no sound in the barn save the mutter of the distant stamps. Then she ran forward, staring at his battered face.

"You're hurt. . . . You—"

"I'm fine." He tried to smile at her. It wasn't easy. The skin about his mouth felt tight, drawn as if it had been stretched too far. "Go on home, and don't tell anyone you were with me last night. It won't help, it will just make trouble for you."

"I've already told Fred Foster and the District Attorney. I tried to make them go down to the saloon and tell the mob. They're both afraid to, said to wait until the men sober up." Contempt made her voice bitter. "I think I'll go down and tell them myself."

"Don't you do that." Bart and Andy said the words at the same time. "Use your head," Andy went on. "Who ever knows what a bunch of drunks may do?"

She said tightly, "I can take care of myself. I never yet saw a man I was afraid of."

Layton cut in, tense. "Sarah, go home and stay out of this. Let me handle it."

"And get yourself killed? You haven't been doing too good a job so far."

"I am not going to get killed. I'll stay out of sight until Judge Anders comes. Then I'm going to Bedford and bring Ryan out. After that, we'll see."

It took a lot of convincing, but she left finally and Layton stretched out again on the hay. But sleep did not come now. His mind turned over and over. What would Hewmark do now? Was Ryan actually insane or merely senile?

Darkness came. Through the cracks in the box stall light flickered as Andy lit the office lantern. Then a team pulled a buggy into the runway. Layton put his eye to a crack between two boards and saw Judge Anders climb tiredly down. Andy came out and they stood for a minute, talking. The judge listened, glancing toward the stall, then came over as Layton pushed open the gate.

"What's all this trouble about, Bart?"

Layton told him quickly, told of his visit to the hospital, of the attack on the hillside, the deaths of the two men. Anders listened intently, especially when Layton told of the offer to buy the mine and his fight with his cousins.

"Don't they realize that any such sale would have to be approved by the court?"

"I didn't know that myself."

"Hewmark should. I suppose he thought that if the three of them came to me I'd approve the order."

"Would you?"

"If I thought it was best for everyone concerned, yes. But you don't think Ryan is insane now?"

"He wasn't when he talked to me. He said he overheard Mary Dorne plotting with Hewmark to steal from the mine. He was furious, which is easy to understand. When you've lived the way Ryan did, when your word has been law for years, to find yourself condemned to a wheelchair and discover that the people who are supposedly taking care of you are robbing you instead . . . I'd hate to guess what I'd do in a like situation."

In the back-light of the lantern Layton could not read Anders' expression, but at least the judge was attentive.

"You should see him." His anger came through. "They tie him to the bed. Can you picture Ryan Layton tied up like a wild animal?"

That thrust reached the judge, and his voice too shook. "That isn't right. But if I do sign the release, suppose he tries to kill the Dorne woman again?"

"He's in a wheelchair, helpless. I guarantee I'll keep him under control."

"All right." Anders' relief was evident. "I'll have to go to the office for the release forms. When do you plan to go after him?"

"As soon as you sign the order."

"The sheriff will have to serve it, you know."

Layton's mouth set. "Then when you sign the paper, hunt up Fred Foster and give it to him and tell him he's going to serve it tonight. If he doesn't, he'll answer to me."

The judge coughed. "Let's not have any more trouble than we need."

"We've got trouble," Layton told him. "I didn't make it, but I'm going to finish it. Just tell Foster that. He knows me; he knows I'll do exactly as I say."

The buildings at Bedford were completely dark. It was nearly two o'clock and Foster was unhappy. Bart Layton was driving the buckboard, and had pushed the horses hard over the curving mountain grade.

Foster's voice was sour, dry. "Doctor Thorpe won't like this at all. Why couldn't we have waited for morning?"

"Because I don't want to." Bart's voice was soft. "I've been pushed around about as much as I mean to be. Montrose was always a Layton town. I'm going to show them that it is again."

He pulled up before the locked gate, got down, used the butt of his gun to hammer on the heavy plates. "Open up. Open up. This is the sheriff."

The guard's sleepy voice came angrily, muffled. "We don't open at night. Come back in the morning."

"You've got two minutes to open that gate, then we start shooting. I told you this is the sheriff."

Foster had stepped down to Layton's side and stood silent, undecided. There was silence from the other side, then a sharp voice called from the main building.

"Richards, what the devil's the racket?"

"The sheriff's here. He wants in."

Thorpe sounded angry. "Foster, is that you?"

Layton had to nudge Fred Foster before he called, "It's me."

"Why?"

"I've got a court order."

"At this time of night?"

"Yes."

Thorpe sounded resigned. "All right, all right, let him in."

There was noise as the bar was withdrawn. The gate swung inward and they stepped forward into the light of the guard's lantern. The guard saw Layton and yelled.

"*You* can't come in."

Layton was taking no chances. He showed the gun already in his hand. "I'm a special deputy. Just behave yourself."

Thorpe read the court order, his face looking yellow under the lamp in the lobby. He looked at Foster, ignoring Layton.

"This is most ill-advised. Very. The man is dangerous . . . a paranoiac."

Fred Foster shrugged. He had accepted the situation and wanted only to be out of it as soon as possible. "That's not up to me, Doctor. The judge signed it. I'm only serving it."

"But surely, it can wait until morning?"

"Surely it cannot," said Bart Layton. The gun he held dominated the room. "I won't leave him in this hell-hole another minute."

Thorpe looked helplessly at the sheriff, then sighed. "Well . . ." He motioned to the guard. "Bring him out."

They made a bed in the back of the buckboard Bart had borrowed from the livery. They turned down the grade, Foster driving. Once clear of the place Bart realized that his grandfather had not uttered a word since he had been wheeled into the receiving room. He twisted on the seat.

"Ryan, are you all right? Warm enough?"

"Course I am," said Ryan Layton. "You take me for a damned invalid?"

Fred Foster grunted. "He sounds about normal at that."

"Course I'm normal, you punk kid. I tried to tell you that when you carted me over here, but you was too busy mooning over that Dorne woman to listen. Maybe it wasn't too good an idea to make you sheriff. Maybe we better get us a new one, next year."

Bart Layton said, "That's enough of that. We've got plenty of trouble without picking fights with friends." He no longer considered Foster a friend, but the man was still sheriff and they were going to need all the help they could get.

His grandfather grunted. "Since when did you start running away from trouble?"

"Maybe I'm beginning to grow up."

Ryan growled. "Don't you go soft on me, boy. That's why I always liked you, you were feisty as a grizzly. Damn a man who won't fight for his rights."

"You had a funny way of showing you liked me."

"What in hell did you want me to do, feed you sugar candy? Sure I picked on you, because I thought you were worth it. The other two were no-good milksops, and I knew it. And I sure found it out for certain after I got hurt. Couldn't depend on them a bit. Had to try to depend on Hewmark and his woman. And they robbed me blind."

"I don't see how they could steal from that mine. Everybody tells me you can't high-grade telluride ore."

"You can steal gold."

Bart Layton glanced toward the sheriff. The moon had come up and he had a clear look at Foster's face. Fred had swiveled his head to look at the old man.

"What do you mean by that?"

"Just what I said. They haul the ore to the mill and run it through the vats and pour it into bars and Hewmark takes every other bar."

"How?"

"Who was to stop him? I couldn't get out of the damned chair. I gave Dick a key to one of the locks to the gold room, but he didn't pay any attention. So they stole half the gold the mine produced, then loaned it back to me as operating capital."

Foster was incredulous. "Do you know this, or are you just guessing?"

Ryan's voice was grim. "I know it. I heard Caleb talking to the woman about it. When he left I jumped her, and she laughed at me, said no one would believe me, that she'd been getting it around that I was going crazy. That's when I got the knife and went for her."

"You could have told someone."

"Told who? I told you, the doctor, the judge, everybody."

"You didn't make much sense. All you did was rave. You couldn't blame us for thinking you'd cracked your mind."

Ryan was silent, then he said in an oddly meek voice, "Could be. It's hell when a man's been running things all his life, and all at once he can't do a damned thing. And got nobody to trust. It's different now. I got Bart. He'll straighten things out."

The voice trailed off. They rode a quiet mile before Bart looked back again. His grandfather was asleep.

Foster cleared his throat uneasily. "What do you

think? Do you suppose they were actually stealing gold, or is it another of his hallucinations?"

"I am going to find out."

"There's another thing. Frank Rudy's going to try to kill you. Oh, I know Sarah Hobart claims you didn't shoot his brother, but—"

"That mob will be sleeping off its drunk by the time we hit town. Before they get steamed up again we can give them something else to think about."

CHAPTER FOURTEEN

Caleb Hewmark, hurrying, rode into town shortly after midnight. He went directly to the doctor's office and beat on the door until he roused the man, demanding, "Dick Layton. Is he here?"

The doctor maintained a semblance of a hospital in his two front rooms. He nodded. "Asleep."

"I've got to talk to him anyhow. How is he?"

The doctor shrugged. He did not like Layton. "He'll live. Got a smashed nose and a couple of cracked ribs. He took quite a beating." Carrying the lamp, he had led Hewmark to the bed in the dark corner.

Both Dick's eyes were swollen nearly shut, there was a bandage against his puffed nose and his voice was hoarse. He answered Hewmark's rapid questions painfully.

145

Hewmark snorted. "We can still force him to sell."

"Not if he gets Ryan out of Bedford. Clint and I won't have an interest in the mine."

This was something Hewmark had not anticipated, but he saw it now. If Ryan Layton assumed management of the Gabriel again the game was lost. He walked with the doctor back to the door.

"Where's the captain?"

The doctor thought he would not tell if he knew. "Frank Rudy had a mob drunk and scouring the town for him. They didn't locate him."

"Are they still looking?"

"They're in bed, I hope. Maybe after they get a little sleep they'll listen to reason."

Hewmark had his own opinion of that. He left and rode back down to the mill. As he reached it he heard a running horse coming up the trail and turned in time to see the guard, McCall, ride up. The Bedford man jumped from the lathered horse, talking as he came.

"That young Layton took his grandfather out tonight. Thorpe sent me to warn you."

Caleb Hewmark swelled with a surging, raging anger. He had planned all this so carefully; he had come so very close. If Bart Layton hadn't come home, he would even now be the owner of the Gabriel.

He said tightly, "Why did Thorpe let him? Why didn't you shoot Layton?"

"The sheriff was with him. They had an order, signed by Judge Anders."

"Have they reached Montrose yet?"

"About five miles out. I rode around them."

"I'll pay a thousand dollars if they never get here."

McCall hesitated, greed riding him, but he shook his head. "If Layton was alone I'd try it. I'm not killing the sheriff. It's too much of a chance."

Hewmark debated. He could climb on his horse and ride the trail himself, maybe get Ryan and Bart Layton and Foster too. But the chances were against his killing both young men, and one left alive, escaping into the darkness, would be dangerous to him.

"All right," he said, "all right." He was not speaking to McCall, he was talking to himself. He turned back to his horse, mounted and rode up the path to the house that had been Ryan Layton's.

Mary Dorne was not asleep. Through the early evening the town below had been noisy with the shouts of drunken men. She heard the horse, then the feet on the porch, then the knock, and Hewmark's well-known voice calling sharply, "Mary. Mary, open up."

She crossed the living room in her nightgown and pulled the door wide. "I tried to wire you in Denver. All hell broke loose here today."

He cut her short. "I know. Layton's bringing Ryan back. He conned that fool judge into signing the order. Tomorrow morning he and Ryan will take control of the mine."

"Oh, no."

"Oh yes. McCall just brought me word."

She said, "I don't think you know this: Frank Rudy has sworn to kill him."

"That isn't going to help us. He got Ryan out, and we'd have one sweet time putting him back in even if Bart Layton were dead."

"You're not going to quit?"

He took her shoulders. "There is about twenty thousand worth of gold in the treasure room, and the hundred thousand I've got hidden in the mine. I was going to ship it to the mint as soon as we took over. Now, I'm going down and collect that gold. At least we'll have that before young Layton moves in."

She retreated to the bedroom, pulling off her nightgown as she went. Hewmark stared at her naked back, puzzled.

"What are you doing?"

"I'm going to find Frank Rudy. Tell him that Layton is coming into town." She dressed rapidly under Hewmark's gaze.

Sarah Hobart had not been sleeping either. Earlier she too had listened to the noise in the town. Every time it became extra loud she went outside, carrying her rifle. She had no idea what she could do, but if the mob caught Layton she meant to try to face them down.

She heard Hewmark's horse, and standing at the window of the darkened room watched him ride up to the Ryan Layton house and hurry through the door. Then she saw him ride down the path, with Mary Dorne following on foot.

Sarah Hobart caught up her rifle and followed the woman, intent on finding out what she was up to.

Mary Dorne did not look behind her. She walked rapidly to the main street and turned along it. Sarah halted at the corner, amazed as she saw Mary Dorne turn in at the saloon. It was the first time she had ever seen a so-called good woman go in through the batwing doors.

She was no more startled than Terry Roark. For him the evening had been pure hell. He had worked silently behind his bar, serving Frank Rudy's rabble as they thronged the long room. Now it was three o'clock and the crowd had faded. Three men had gone to sleep on the floor at the rear; Frank and one die-hard sat at a poker table, staring at nothing, stupified by liquor.

Terry Roark started around the end of the bar but Mary was already past, crossing to the table. Frank Rudy caught her movement and looked up. He was still half drunk, although Roark had refused to refill his glass more than an hour before.

He blinked, his muddled brain telling him that no woman had any business in this room. But before he could rise Mary Dorne was beside him, saying tightly, "You're looking for Bart Layton. He's driving in on the Bedford road, bringing his grandfather with him."

Rudy shook his head, trying to focus his mind. The words sobered him as nothing else would have. He fumbled to his feet, knocking over his chair. The other man at the table came up with him, steadier than Rudy.

"So. So. Let's go get him."

They brushed past Mary Dorne, on a half run for the door. Terry Roark moved to stop them, but the woman got in his way, so that he missed them.

He said bitterly, "I hope you know what you've done."

The urge flitted through her to yell at him, "I've just stolen the Gabriel."

She did not. She ran to the street, where Rudy had stopped, belatedly wanting more information. He swung on her.

"How many men with Layton?"

She did not want to tell him about the sheriff. "I don't know. He's probably alone."

The second man belched. "Maybe I'd better round up some of the boys."

"No time." Mary sounded urgent. "He should be here any minute. If you want to catch him on the trail before he gets in town you'd better find some horses and get going."

Rudy scrubbed his hands through his mop of hair as if to scratch his brain awake, then ran toward the livery, the second man trotting behind.

Sarah Hobart had come quietly forward, keeping in the shadow of the building front. She was within fifteen feet when Rudy turned away from Mary. She called, "Wait a minute, you."

The new voice bewildered them and they stopped. Things were happening a little too fast for their liquor-fevered brains.

"You're out to get Bart Layton. You're after the wrong person. He didn't kill your brother."

Mary Dorne had been as startled by the appearance of the younger girl as the men were. Her impulse was to shout at the Hobart girl to mind her own business, but she waited too long. Rudy was already demanding angrily, "What do you know about it?"

"Everything," said Sarah. "Bart Layton did not kill your brother. I did."

It was like the explosion of a bomb.

The three of them gaped at her in disbelief. At length Rudy hitched his trousers and sneered.

"I don't know why you want to protect Layton, but it won't do him any good. I ain't buying the story."

Her voice was contempt. "Then you're even a bigger fool than I thought. You're being used by this woman. She has to get rid of Layton so she and Hewmark can steal the Gabriel."

"You don't make sense. What would all that have to do with my brother, even if it was so? And why should you shoot him?"

"Because he was a no-good, thieving bum who'd hired out to kill Bart Layton and was shooting at him from ambush when I fired."

"Why you little bitch . . . I've watched the way you sashay around this town. . . . If your father can't handle you, by damn, I can." He took two quick steps toward her.

"Get back." The rifle came up.

Frank Rudy did not believe she would shoot. He made a grab for her. The light rifle sent its single explosion through the night.

The bullet struck Rudy full in the mouth. He stopped as if he had run into an invisible wall. He dropped, his body crumpling until it lay a twisted, inert form in the shadowed dust of the street.

The man behind him stared at the girl, hardly trusting his senses, then with a yell he spun and ran up the sidewalk as if the demons of hell were on his coattails.

Mary Dorne was frozen, stunned for seconds, then she said in a barely audible, stifled whisper, "You killed him . . . you killed the man. . . ."

Sarah Hobart looked at her without visible feeling. "Somebody had to. Maybe it would be better if someone killed you."

Mary gasped, her eyes wide on the small figure, the leveled rifle. Then she too flung around and raced away.

Half a mile below town Layton and Fred Foster heard the single rifle shot. The sheriff whipped the team and they spun into town to find Terry Roark standing beside Sarah in front of the saloon. Foster dropped from the buckboard and ran toward them. In the light falling from the saloon window he saw Rudy's still body, saw the rifle in the girl's hands. Roark did not give him time to ask questions.

"Rudy jumped her," he said. "She didn't have any choice. She shot in self-defense. I saw it."

Layton had come up in time to hear as the bartender went on.

"They were fixing to bushwhack you, Bart. Sarah told them she was the one who killed Rudy's brother, but they still meant to get you."

Fear for the girl made Layton's voice rough. "I told you to go home and stay there."

"If I had, you'd be dead." She showed no emotion. She lifted her head and started up the street, then stopped, looking back. "Hewmark came an hour ago. He went up the hill to the Dorne woman. She was the one who told Rudy you were coming."

"How did they find out?"

"I don't know that."

"Where's Hewmark now?"

"Last I saw, he was going toward the mill."

He stepped toward her, saying, "Look, I've got to get Ryan to the hotel, I don't want to leave him alone, and I've got to find Hewmark before he starts anything else. Do me a favor, will you? Stay with Ryan?"

She did not hesitate. "Sure."

At the buckboard Ryan Layton was awake, sputtering in curiosity. "What's going on? What's all the argument?"

Bart said, "Frank Rudy just got himself killed."

"Did, huh? He always was hardheaded."

Bart lifted out the wheelchair, lifted his grandfather into it, and spoke to the girl. "Can you handle this thing?"

They went to the hotel together, she pushing the chair over the rough walk, he with his gun in his hand, watching for any further trouble.

The shot had awakened the clerk, who stood just inside the lobby, watching through the window. He pulled open the door and wordlessly let them in.

Layton said, "I need a couple of rooms, with a door between them if possible."

The clerk's eyes were lively with curiosity, but saying nothing, he reached for keys and carried a lamp up the stairs. Layton carried his grandfather up and in the corner room laid him on the bed. As he turned to leave the old man spluttered querulously again. "Now where the hell you going?"

"To have a showdown with Hewmark."

"That will hold till morning."

Bart Layton shook his head, not wanting to stop and explain his fear that Hewmark would take off with what gold there was in the treasure room of the mill. In the hall outside he told Sarah in a low voice, "Just stay in the next room. If he got the idea you were guarding him I don't know what he'd try."

"You expect them to try to get to him?"

"I don't know what to expect. I only know I owe you a great deal and that you're the only person in Montrose I can trust."

She watched him leave, thinking, *he'll be killed,* and suddenly could not stand the thought. She put out a hand, started to call his name, then did not. He had already disappeared down the stairs.

CHAPTER FIFTEEN

The mill was nearly deserted. Bart Layton came into the office to find the manager, Allen, alone, starting as if he saw a ghost.

"You . . . I thought you were dead."

"Why?"

"That's what Hewmark said. He came in here like a wild man, said Frank Rudy and a mob had caught and lynched you and were going to burn the mill and wreck the mine. He said he had to get the gold out to a safe place."

"Did he have Dick's key? How did he get into the room?"

The man wrung his hands. "I helped him break down the door, helped him load the bars into the wagon."

"How come you're still here?"

"I thought, when the mob came, maybe I could talk them out of burning the place."

Layton was already running toward the store room. The door was sagging open, splintered by an ax. The room was empty. He ran back to the manager.

"Where did Hewmark go?"

"To the mine, he said. He told me he had to get some records out of the office before Rudy's crowd wrecked it."

Layton jumped for the door and ran up the street, seeing a light in Foster's office as he passed the courthouse. He almost paused for help, then did not. He could not trust the sheriff in this.

The mine had a sadly deserted look. But a lamp burned in the shaft house and a wagon was drawn up before the small building at the top of the dump. Then Tom Hobart came to the lighted doorway as he heard Layton's pounding steps. He looked as startled as Allen had.

"I heard you were dead—"

"Hewmark?"

156

The miner nodded.

"He's wrong. Where is he?"

"Below."

Impatience rode up into Layton's voice. "Below where?"

"At the fourth level. At least that's where the lift is. He took it down." Hobart pointed to an indicator on the shaft house wall. The needle pointed to four.

"What's down there?"

"Nothing supposed to be." Hobart shrugged. "That level was abandoned two years ago. We built a bulkhead door to block it off."

"Then why would Hewmark go there?"

Hobart hesitated, then said unwillingly, "I guess he's after the gold."

"What gold?" Layton caught the man's shoulder and shook it roughly.

Hobart wiped at his mouth with the back of his hand. "Why, the gold bars that are hid down there."

"How much is there? What do you know about it? Talk fast, man."

The miner was still reluctant, halting. "I don't know . . . a lot . . . I got curious one night so when no one was around I took off the hinges to have a look. . . ."

"Why didn't you tell anyone?"

"Who would I tell? Your cousins? They wouldn't have believed me, wouldn't even have come to look. Hewmark was running the mine. If he wanted to hide gold it was his business."

"You could have told me."

"I didn't know you. I didn't know how you'd take to it."

"Can you bring up the lift?"

"Sure . . . but if I do Hewmark will know something's happened."

"Right. Get me a light. Do you have a gun here?"

"Shotgun." The miner nodded toward the double barreled gun on a bracket against the wall, and went for a miner's lamp.

Layton followed, saying, "I'm going to climb down. If Hewmark should pass me coming up, hold him here until I can get back."

The man groaned. "Captain, I just don't want any part of this."

"You want to keep working?"

"Well . . ."

"I brought Ryan Layton home last night. From now on he and I are running the Gabriel. Do as I tell you and you've still got a job. Don't, and you can start walking out of Montrose now."

He did not wait for an answer. They were at the shelf where the row of lamps sat. He adjusted one, fastened it to a cap and put the cap on his head. Then he moved to the ladder, the emergency exit from the depths below.

The levels were spaced fifty feet apart. The shaft was a three compartment affair, one for the lift in which the miners rode from the surface to their work area, one for the huge scoop that hoisted the newly mined ore from the haulage drifts. The third was used to pump water out of the mine. It was down one side of this that the ladder ran.

Layton looked down into it and saw only black dark. He must descend two hundred feet, with only the little flame on the cap to guide him. He put a foot on the top rung and discovered it to be slippery as a slug with the slime of dampness.

He clung to the handrail and eased himself down, setting each foot firmly before trusting his weight to it. He reached the first level and paused, looking around the twenty by thirty station hacked out of the solid rock. Then he eased on. His fear, and it was a real one, was that a rung would be missing or would give under him.

At the second level he paused again, to look and listen. Dripping water was the only sound. The whole network of the mine was otherwise as silent as a grave. Even the roar of the blowers which ventilated the mine when the crews were working was stilled.

The darkness felt smothering as he went on. Without the blowers the air had a stale, metallic taste. His chest tightened with the cold touch of panic and he fought against gasping for breath.

He passed the third level and peered into the stygian blank below, looking for a sign of Hewmark's lamp. He saw nothing and left his own burning. It was taking a chance that the other man would see his tiny glow and be warned, but the chance was offset for him by the danger of trying to feel his way in the gloom.

He reached the station of the fourth, the abandoned level and stepped onto the solid rock floor with a flood of relief. He was sweating. Without the blowers the air was hot, stifling, but he knew it was his nerves that made him perspire. He was keyed up. He could not recall any time when he had been so tense.

He pulled his gun from its holster and looked around the chamber. The lift with its half gate raised hung at the level of the floor and he saw the stack of bars already loaded on it. Eight bars. He did not know how much each was worth, but it was a relief to see them. Ryan was right. There could be no question that Hewmark had been stealing from the mine. There was no other explanation why these bars should have been hidden in the unused drift.

The Gabriel, then, was making money. It should continue to make money. The mine need not close. The town would not die. Thought of the town's future made him think of Sarah. She had had faith, courage, more courage than anyone he had ever met. She would be far more relieved that Montrose would live than he.

But he found that the town's fate had become important to him too.

And then his ear caught the click of a boot nail on stone.

The bulkhead, as was usual, had been built across the abandoned tunnel. The heavy plank door hung open. Layton quickly extinguished his light and groped through the darkness that swiftly shut in around him. He found the bulkhead, felt along it to the door and peered around the casing.

Far down the tunnel he saw the pinpoint of Hewmark's light. It moved slowly toward him. He saw the man first as a shadow under the lamp, then the figure took shape. He was carrying a gold bar and judging by the way he walked it was heavy.

Layton waited with an eerie feeling, with nothing breaking the stillness save the impersonal drip of water and the shuffling of Hewmark's boots, with the knowledge that in all the miles of underground workings which were the Gabriel there were only the two of them. They were as cut off from the normal world as though they were on another planet.

The man reached the doorway. He stepped through, not seeing Layton, standing pressed tightly against the bulkhead to the left of the opening. Hewmark walked by, then Layton took a step toward him and jammed his gun into the man's back, hard.

"Careful. I'd be glad of an excuse to kill you."

Hewmark stopped. He showed no surprise; he

did not speak. He stood quiet, still holding the heavy bar.

Layton used his free hand to get Hewmark's gun. He flipped it across the room. It caught a glint of light, then arced over the brink of the haulage compartment of the shaft. Seconds later a splash echoed up as it hit the water in the sump.

Layton prodded with his gun. "Go on. To the lift."

They moved forward together, passing a stack of rusting tools against the station wall. Just before he would reach the lift, Hewmark stumbled. He fell sideways, against the wall, brushing the lamp from his cap as he went down. The room was doused into blackness so deep it felt solid.

Layton fired at where he thought the man lay. He fired again and yet a third time. The gun's echoes ricocheted around the rock walls with deafening force.

There was dense silence then. Layton stood perfectly still, holding his breath, listening for the other's breathing. He did not know whether he had hit Hewmark, nor where he was.

Suddenly out of the inky blackness Hewmark rushed him, guided by the flash of the gun. A shoulder struck him in the chest, knocked him back against the ragged wall, jarred the gun from his hand. Then something crashed against the wall close by his head. Iron on stone, striking bright sparks. He guessed that Hewmark had grabbed up a miner's short-handled pick from the pile of tools.

He dropped, crawling blindly along the wall, felt among the tools and found a pick for himself. He came up to his feet quietly, yet his pick clinked against another tool.

He heard Hewmark's rush toward the sound. He raised his pick to stop the rush and felt it strike something soft. Then Hewmark was clawing at him with one hand. It gripped his upper arm, slid down, fastened on his wrist like a vise.

As Layton fought to break free Hewmark swung his pick, aiming for Layton's face. He missed by a little. The point went by, the handle cracked against the shoulder and numbed the entire arm.

With a violent jerk Layton tore his wrist from Hewmark's clutch and jumped away, circling the room with soft steps, trying for time to regain the use of the hand. He must, he knew, keep a sense of direction, keep clear of the yawning mouth of the shaft. Yet in the blackness how could he? Only, he thought, by keeping contact with the wall.

It was a weird and hellish way to fight. Two men in total darkness, each intent to hear sound from the other, circling, guessing when to swing, when to move.

Twice his pick hit Hewmark. He heard the man's curse, then the flat side of Hewmark's pick slammed against Layton's head and dropped him to his knees. Lights flashed behind his eyes. He felt for the wall and could not find it. He did not know which way it was.

Hewmark sensed that he was down. He surged forward, using the pick as a scythe, searching ahead with wide sweeping blows. Layton felt the air move close to him as the tool swung by. He flattened himself against the wet rock floor. He heard the pick swing inches above his head, reached out through the blackness, caught Hewmark's legs, brought the man down on top of him.

He rolled, trying to get out from under. Hewmark scrabbled desperately for his throat, found it and locked his powerful fingers around the windpipe and clung there, staying on Layton's back.

Desperation gave Layton strength he did not know he had. He heaved upward, managed to get to his hands and knees. Then, arching, threw the heavier man over his head. The strangling grip broke.

He stayed where he was, his gasping lungs sucking in the hot acrid air. Then he was up, groping, turning, reaching out, feeling for either Hewmark or the wall.

His hands touched cloth first. He dragged the resisting body toward him, wrapped both arms about the middle and squeezed him in, wanting to crush the rib cage.

Hewmark spun, breaking loose, retreating, fumbling with his feet for the fallen pick.

Layton followed the sounds. Then there came a

high, wild cry of shock and terror. It filled the station, echoed like a banshee wail, fading, growing hollow. Then, far below, the sound of a great splash.

Layton froze where he was. Cold swept through him. He was turned around. He had lost his direction. Only by a miracle it was not he who had stumbled over the edge into the shaft and plunged the ten levels to the dark waters of the sump.

He stood swaying, trying to fill his lungs, to still his racing heart. Then he felt through his pocket, struck a match. He used three before he found his cap and lamp. He lit it and breathed more easily. He carried it to the brink of the shaft. He could see nothing in the shrouding blackness. He listened, but heard no sound of struggle below, heard nothing.

He backed away. His cheek felt sticky and he put a hand to it. Blood oozed from a long gash where the pick's dull bit had torn the skin. Another inch and it might have chewed through, broken his jaw. He shivered. He had been up against guns, Apache lances, knives—but a man swinging a pick at his face. . . .

He put the picture away, turned back into the drift from which Hewmark had carried the gold bar. The tunnel was over half a mile long. He walked the length clear to the face and found no sign of other bars. Either Hewmark had brought out the last one or they had not been hidden in the drift proper.

Above it and to one side, following the pitch of the vein, the mountain had been stoped up, the stopes filled with square sets, timbers supporting working platforms, arranged like the cells of a beehive, so that each level supported the next one up. From these platforms the miners knocked down ore from the roof, dropping it into the loading chutes which would dump it on the haulage carts below.

Layton climbed to the first platform, searched it without success, climbed higher and found the cache of bars. He carried them one at a time back to the lift, and when the last was loaded he rang the bell for Hobart to hoist him to the shaft house.

Hobart was holding the shotgun in the crook of his arm when Layton's head rose above the ground level. From his black face he expected Hewmark, and was prepared to carry out Layton's order. He stared at Bart's battered, bloody face and sucked his breath sharply between his teeth.

"Where's Hewmark?"

"He fell in the sump. Help me get these out to the wagon." He indicated the stack of bars.

He was surprised when he went outside to find that it was daylight. He stepped tiredly to the driver's seat and with Hobart beside him drove the team down to the banker's house. He waked

166

Heath while Hobart stayed on the wagon, still clutching the shotgun.

"Come on," he told the banker. "I want to borrow your safe. It was too hard to get this gold back to take the chance of losing it again."

CHAPTER SIXTEEN

From behind the livery Mary Dorne watched Layton and the sheriff come into town. She saw Layton take his grandfather to the hotel, then leave and head for the mill. He reappeared minutes later, running toward the mine.

Curiosity and foreboding drove her to the mill. Allen was not pleased to see her and his answers were short, but she guessed what must have happened and climbed the street to take up a position from which she could watch the shaft house.

She was still there when Layton and Hobart carried out the gold and hauled it to the banker's house. She did not know what had happened in the mine, but Hewmark must be dead. He would never otherwise relinquish that fortune.

She came back along the street in time to see Hobart and Layton carry the treasure into the bank, then followed Layton as he made his way once more to the hotel.

Already she had decided what she must do. It

never entered her head to simply give up. She had had her dream too long.

Layton did not pause in the lobby, but swung quickly up the stairs and along the hall to his grandfather's door. She ran after him lightly and called from the top step.

"Captain, I want to talk to you."

He stopped, turned, his face creasing with surprise. He did not want to talk to her, alone. He pushed the door open and started in. The bed was empty, the wheelchair gone. Sarah had had the old man taken down to breakfast.

Mary Dorne pushed in behind him and closed the door, saying breathlessly, "I don't know what you think of me—"

He shrugged. He had no interest. She was a very attractive woman, but a dangerous one. He sensed the latent drive, the unfaltering determination.

She did not give him time to answer. "I came to make a deal. I suppose Caleb is dead?"

"He fell down the shaft."

She was looking at his hard, marked face. "Fell or was pushed." Her tone was indifferent.

He let it pass.

"I said I want to make a deal. There is one hundred thousand dollars in Hewmark's account at the Denver bank. He meant to use it as a down payment on the Gabriel. It came from stolen gold."

"Why tell me?" He watched her, trying to guess her new game.

"Because the account is in Hewmark's name. I have no way of claiming it. He's got a sister somewhere who will inherit unless you bring court action to recover."

"And your deal?"

"I'll go into court and tell the whole story of Hewmark's attempt to take over the mine. I'll swear that the Denver money belongs to the Gabriel. In return, I want half of that money, fifty thousand dollars."

He laughed shortly, without mirth. "I do have to admire gall, ma'am. But my answer is no. Even if I were inclined to let you get away with it, the decision isn't mine. It's Ryan's. And the way he feels about you, he'd never consent to your putting your hands on one nickel."

"You are a fool, Captain. You need my cooperation."

He shook his head. "I don't think we do. With Hobart's and Allen's testimony I think we can establish that Hewmark had been systematically looting the property for two years, that the money belongs to us. Thank you for telling me about it. We can learn whom he sold the gold to and check the dates of deposits."

She stared at him, her eyes smoky. "All right, Captain, you may force me to use a woman's weapon. Unless I get what I want I will ruin you—in a way that a woman can be certain of ruining a man. I can tear off my clothes and start screaming.

When the people in the dining room rush up here
. . . and they will . . . I will be naked. I will swear
that you tried to rape me. Just think about it. A
lot of Frank Rudy's friends were ready to hang
you last night. They still aren't convinced you
didn't kill Frank. And if I yell rape—"

"You won't. You'd ruin yourself."

"What have I got to lose? Besides, they'd feel
sorry for me. You don't know men the way I do.
You have one minute, Captain. Either I get fifty
thousand dollars or you'll never be able to live in
this town. Believe me."

He looked at her in helpless uncertainty. She
lifted her hand, caught the collar of her shirtwaist
and ripped the cloth down, exposing the under-
garment, a bare shoulder and the swell of her
rising breast.

"Do I scream?"

A voice behind them said, "I wouldn't. It's
going to be hard to convince your audience that
even as vital a man as Captain Layton would try
to rape one woman when he already has one in
bed."

They swung around. Sarah Hobart was sitting
up in Ryan's bed, the covers hugged up to cover
her breasts, but both shoulders were bare. There
was no doubt that she was at least half naked.

Mary Dorne gasped. "You! Where did you come
from?"

"I've been here, waiting."

She was lying, Bart knew. The bed had been empty when he came into the room. He glanced toward the connecting door that led to Sarah's room. It was ajar.

Mary Dorne did not know what to believe. She had paid no attention to the bed, had been too intent on her mission with Layton. Something was going on here that she didn't understand.

"Damn you." Her voice rasped. "You're always in the way, always spying. God damn you." She clutched her torn blouse together with one hand. She opened the door with the other. She slammed it hard behind her.

Bart Layton began to laugh. He could not remember laughing so hard in his whole life. It hurt the bruises, the healing scabs of his face. But he could not stop. He sank on the edge of the bed, holding his sides. He gasped, trying to talk.

"Did you . . . ever see anything . . . as . . . funny . . . as her face? God!" He twisted to the girl in the bed, who now held the covers up under her chin as a wall between them. "Where did you come from at that? You weren't here when I first opened the door."

There was no amusement in her tone. "I saw you, from the dining room, then I saw her chasing after you. I knew she'd make some kind of trouble, so I came up to my room and listened. When I heard what she was threatening I couldn't resist undressing and slipping in here. You two

171

were so busy shouting at each other that you didn't see me."

His laughter was still pulsing, surging. "You're a coot. You're crazy. Nobody but you would think of doing such a thing. First you save my life, then you kill the man who wanted to lynch me, and now you sacrifice your honor to protect mine." His laughter overtook him again, pealing higher than ever.

She got mad. "What's so funny about that?"

"Nothing . . . nothing, it's just—the way you do everything."

"From the looks of your face your way of doing things isn't so smooth. Hewmark marked you plenty. Did he really fall, or did you knock him into the shaft?"

"He fell. I wasn't near him."

"And now you're going to run the mine."

"I'm going to help Ryan run it. The mine's still rich."

"And Ryan will see that you run it right. So the town's all right. People won't have to move away."

"The town's fine. We'll keep it that way."

"May I ask you one question?"

"A hundred. I'll try to answer them all."

"Why did you get fired from the army?"

He laughed again. "I hit the general."

"You hit the general?" She was incredulous.

"Why not? He's no bigger than I am."

"It's you that's outlandish, not me. Nobody hits a general."

"I did. I guess we'll make a good pair."

Her eyes widened. "Now what are you talking about?"

"Well, I guess it's my turn to save your honor. By the time that cat gets through spreading her story everybody in Montrose will think we've been sleeping together ever since I came home."

"Now, wait one minute, Captain. I am not going to marry you. I'm not marrying any fool man who thinks he has to make me honest. When I get married it will be because the man respects me and loves me, the way I love him."

"Sarah, I *do* . . ."

"You don't even know me."

He was grinning, enjoying baiting her, enjoying her quick reactions. "Look, I won't have any choice when your father gets the news. He'll come gunning for me with his shotgun."

"Pooh. My father quit a long time ago."

"That's what you think. He's a different man this morning. Right now he's sitting down at the bank with that shotgun, watching the safe."

She shook her head vigorously. "It doesn't matter. I wouldn't marry you if three people were shooting at you."

He stood up with mock gravity. He started to unbutton his shirt. Her eyes widened again.

"What are you up to now?"

"I learned how to force a deal. Either you promise to marry me or I'm getting into bed with you. I've heard that rape has a way of changing a woman's mind."

"You wouldn't dare."

He continued to pull off his shirt.

Suddenly she moved, throwing back the covers. She was a white streak of nakedness, leaping from the bed, diving for the connecting door. It slammed after her and he heard the bolt shoot into place.

He did not go after her. He collapsed on the edge of the bed again, helpless in the spasm of laughter. Nothing in his experience had prepared him for Sarah Hobart. She was unique. The only one.

Let her get her clothes on, let her regather her dignity. There would be time enough to work on her, to convince her that he needed her for more than emergency help. That was the pattern of her that had revealed itself to him. Sarah Hobart wanted, needed, to be needed.

Center Point Large Print
600 Brooks Road / PO Box 1
Thorndike, ME 04986-0001 USA

(207) 568-3717

US & Canada:
1 800 929-9108
www.centerpointlargeprint.com